BREACH OF TRUST

BREACH OF TRUST

A Tale of Asheville in the Civil War

Philip J. Tate

*This Book is Dedicated
To
Sharon McKinney Godfrey
For the work of 59
Years association
With my family*

Secession in Asheville

It was early winter, just before Christmas in Asheville, 1860, and the leaves from the town mountains were blowing between the buildings on the street as the wind made a force tunnel as it blew between the buildings such that it intensified speed and cold and everything. The sun was shining through low-moving clouds, and patches of blue were showing through. As Susan stepped out into the street, her long hair blowing in the wind, she sheltered her face with her scarf, and though she had a nice overcoat on, she drew her arms to her chest to fend off the cold. She had an errand to run for the bank to a law office off a little side street, and it wouldn't take long but was of master importance. Things were fixing to change. The politics between North and South had become fractious. Lawyers with safes were banking for the banks now, storing their gold privately for when secession came, and the currency changed.

Susan hustled to the office with the note: On it was simply a time. But it was an important time, for it was the time that the gold would be transferred in the dark of night to the law office under guard and in one load. There was not to be back and forth nor double loading. It was to be all at once. Susan held the note in her gloved fist for dear life and run she did. It was about 2:00 in the afternoon, and due to the wind, not many people were stirring on the street. However, had there been, Susan would have turned heads, as she likely was the prettiest 27-year-old banker in Western North Carolina.

Now Susan made it to the little obscure law office occupied by Johnson, Wipple, Taylor and Young. This was the oldest law firm in Asheville and dealt with banks and private clients very discreetly and confidentially. There was no gold leaf on the window. Not even a shingle. One would have to be introduced to the firm through personal referral and then be vetted for representation. Once committed, the firm's lawyers teamed up on the case till success was achieved. Quietly and without fanfare, Susan stepped inside and Miss Fanny, the receptionist. welcomed her in a friendly business way and ushered her into the office of Alan Johnson, Esq. Senior partner in the firm. Lawyer Johnson, dressed to the nines in the manner of all prosperous lawyers, greeted Susan and pulled back a chair for her to sit and warm up close to the heater stove. Johnson could appreciate beauty when he saw it, and he acknowledged Susan, giving her time to relax for a minute. Susan handed him the note. January 15th, 1861, 2:00 am, it read. He already knows the time. Johnson offered Susan some honeyed tea and crackers for refreshment, which she took gladly, and they made small talk while she refreshed herself. Susan had come from an established pre- revolutionary family in Asheville. Her last name was Jackson, and her father dealt in real estate and second mortgages and had stock in the local banks at the time. In short, Susan had some pull, had been a debutante and was well thought of. Once refreshed, Susan thanked Mr. Johnson and said she had better get back to the bank. She told Miss Fanny bye and opened the door to head back up the walk to the bank, the bitter wind hitting her in the face.

The bank was busy when Susan came in through the lobby and went to the office of the President, Eunicile Webster. She simply said, "It's done," and went back to her office, poured a cup of coffee and attempted to take a breath and warm up before she needed to begin to balance the morning's work from the tellers. "Oh yes, today is November 2nd ", she thought as she savored the coffee and got organized to begin balancing. Tonight, at church, was choir practice and hopefully a dessert with Paul, her beau of six years. Paul was a deputy sheriff who had been on the force since he was 18 and, at 29, now was getting restless for greener pastures: possibly the State Bureau, but with secession talk and the uncertainty of State Administration, he might as well wish for the Texas Rangers. The future was looking mighty obscure. "What sort of government will we have? "he wondered... is it going to be the amateur hour or a group of professionals? Hard to say." Paul remembered he had a dessert and coffee date with Susan, and he quit wondering about the politics of the State and much else for the day.

Meanwhile, the cheap talk of Saber rattling was rampant in Charleston and Columbia, South Carolina. Lincoln had sent troops to Fort Sumpter and enraged Southerners were ginning themselves up for a fight. Meantime, those in the know around Asheville and the Southeast, for that matter, were preparing to protect their wealth, and the days marched on until it became the night of January 15th, 1861.

Susan had actually forgotten that this was the day for whatever President Webster was having done at the Law Office today. Susan balanced her work, and the staff left, and Mr. Webster said he would stay, for he had work to do and would lock up the vault. So off marched the bank staff, including Susan. The only light left on in the bank was Webster's office, and there was a lamp on a table by the front door.

At exactly 2:00 AM, a team pulled up with a heavy wagon on the side door of the bank, and five men entered through the unlocked door, met Webster and began hauling large bags of gold coinage out of the vault while other men replaced identical bags of punk metal coin in their place.

Moving quietly and swiftly, the wagon went the block and a half and left turn into the back door of the law office, where Mr. Johnson met them and led them to the large double-door safe where they deposited the gold. These men were paid for their troubles not in gold but in dollars and then told to disappear. Mr. Johnson set the lock and walked home across the bridge to Flint Street. The common folk of Asheville slept, unaware that the equity had been moved. But certain wealthy people knew. It was not a week before South Carolina fired on Ft. Sumter and announced then the Vote of Succession. States followed.

Just after, across the western mountains, a single wagon pulled by heavy oxen penetrated Soco Gap. Its cargo was loaded on a barge on the river and floated into a wet cave only known to Lawyer Johnson and a

Cherokee warrior Sewakahony. The wagon was broken up for fire kindling and the gold was buried in the cave deep. The Indian walked upriver and crossed at the first ford. Silence would be golden now. The gold was secured, at least for now.

A confederacy arose from the dust of the temperate battles, and the war talk rang out. A new currency was printed at the Asheville Bank. Suzie was involved in the administration of the transfer, and paper backed by punk-metal was the deal of the day for Asheville's most popular bank. It would be no surprise to anyone that Susan's dad, Mr. Stanford Jackson, was a director of the Asheville Bank and was a client of the law firm of Johnson, Wipple, Taylor, and Young. He and members of the firm bought and sold real estate together. Financing their deals through the bank is typical of Southern small-town doings.

The question was, who knew about this transfer of the gold? Webster, Johnson, wagon driver, the Indian Sewakahony. Did Susan's dad, Stanford Jackson, know or any of the directors? Was this an approved move or an embezzlement by Bank President Webster and Lawyer Johnson? Surely, it would have been prudent to protect the gold, considering all the war talks. But who's authorization, if any? The fact was that Johnson, Wipple, Taylor, and Young were not the bank representing attorneys. Who was behind this? Only time would tell.

Meantime, the war talk raged. People began to hoard back food and other supplies. Not as much gold coinage was coming into the bank from the public as they were stashing elsewhere. Prices began going up on goods related to transportation, horses, wagons, tack, feed, and shoes for both man and beast. In civic organization, the men spoke of the politics of succession, and militias were informally established even before the war news came. But finally, the hot-headed South Carolinians fixated on Fort Sumter, and it was on. Asheville stopped seemingly as the small-town city that it was and took a breath. The preachers prayed and the upper echelon financers were looking way ahead to protect their fortunes and make money where they could off the conflict to come. In all of this, Susan, though anxious, stuck to her knitting, so to speak, at the bank. The Jackson had commercial rental property all over the Asheville area and Black Mountain to Waynesville, and their interest wasn't only in commercial real estate, for that matter, and their interest wasn't only in commercial real estate but in farmland and timber and mining interests of copper ore. And yes, the family held slaves to work on all this real estate, farming, timbering, and mining. The fact was that the Jacksons likely held the top third slaves in the region. They were well housed and fed and were not bedrugged nor were beaten. They are employed for their sustenance. That, however, did not make it right. It was just a fact. An investment in the overall program they were. Susan had grown up with it, and it was a fact of life for her. She was isolated from the work of the farms, timberland, and mining interests for the family, who had a fine house in town not far from the First Baptist Church and within walking distance from the bank and all the city's amenities. Susan had grown up, particularly of some wealth, schooled at the local girls' finishing school, and then made the obligatory trip to Europe, where she went on adventures, seeing the capitals and rounding out her education.

Susan had a younger sister, Ellen, and a younger brother, John Donald Jackson, named after his grandfather. These young people were among the centerpieces of the families growing up supposedly on the right side of the tracks of Asheville city proper.

Susan, however, went back to the bank from her errand to the law office and mused about this evening with choir practice and the after-practice dessert social with Paul coming at heart for a while, for he was on shift and would have to leave early. Paul had been seeing Susan for some time, and her dad Stanford thought he was okay, but Susan's mother, Joan Fontain Jackson, of New Orleans origin, thought she could do better. Susan's dad, Stanford, figured he could help eventually get the boy the Sheriff's post if they tied the knot, but the French aristocracy in Joan Fontain's blood was seeking higher social class and wealth for her daughter. It was bad enough to have left French New Orleans for the backwater town of Asheville, but she also had to compromise her Catholicism to attend the Baptist Church with her husband and family, though she had a rosary and a Mary's statue in her bedroom. She was a going Baptist but a practicing Catholic.

Susan wound up her work on that day and met her friend Kathy Generese for supper at a diner up on the square, just a block from the bank, it was only a short walk to the Baptist Church where they were going to choir practice. Susan had grown up in the Church with Kathy, and they had gone to school together. Her father, Spencer Generese, ran a mercantile grocery and butcher's shop just over the hill from the square, and he was highly successful as city folk did big trade with him. Farmers brought produce to sell to him wholesale, and Susan's father provided beef, pork, and veal. Asheville then was a very much (I'll scratch your back, you'll scratch mine) town where mutual cooperation helped all prosper on the upper echelon of line money. The slave economy, however unrighteous it was, kept those who benefited fifty-four percent profitable to start. The monied elite of Asheville was split on the issue of succession because they didn't want the disruption of their system and knew that war would bring them deprivation and hardship. Kathy and Susan had a blue plate special at the diner and had a little time to visit before choir. Their usual subject was boys and fashion, generally in that older. Kathy had a boyfriend named Kenneth Lee Othario, who was a horseman extraordinaire and had stables and livery, rented buggies and bought and sold tack and horses. He dabbled on the racing side. He was of Italian ancestry, as you would figure Generese would simply imply too, and yet he served the rich and the poor with needed transportation at fair prices. Kathy and Kenneth were engaged to be married but in no hurry, as their relationship seemed solid, and it might be a year before Kenneth would be able to give Kathy's dad a worthy dowry for Kathy's hand. Her father, Spencer, liked Ken and appreciated his industry and hard work. As Kenneth provided him with a horse tack and buggy for grocer delivery, there again, cooperation brought loyalty. The girls, Kathy and Susan, window-shopped on their way to Church. Prices had gone up on fine dresses and gowns as a war succession talk had already begun to impact the economy. Getting to Church, they filled in their places in the choir, and the practice was full of hymns such as *Onward Christian Soldiers* and *Abide With Me*. The girls sang but had their minds on the refreshment reception afterward. This was a reception for the whole church, and the women folk had put out a formal spread. It glittered with crystal and silver, and the candlelight gave it some romance even though it was to be a Church social. Kathy and Susan helped a little and waited by the door for their beaus, with Kenneth being the first to arrive. He had cleaned up at the stables and changed clothes and was striking in his demeanor, the Italian good looks shining through. Paul was late, but he came in explaining that he had been called to the Cherokee reservation to help investigate the murder of a Buncombe County man who had been missing for some time and was found buried in a ravine off the road in Soco Gap, stricken in the back of the neck by an axe and buried, what was odd, was he was buried with some due respect wrapped in buckskin, arms crossed with coins over his eyes and an eagle feather lying on his chest under the crossed arms. The murder had been clean and efficient, one blow to the back of the neck. Nothing was messy, and there was no fight. Susan and Paul had to put the subject down for the time of the little reception, and he spoke of it no more that evening, but it was hard. The couples took refreshments and made small talk pausing to greet all their elders, as is the southern custom now and was in their day. The Baptists did not dance then, but there was religious chamber music, and it was a nice evening, as Paul had to get back to his shift; he offered to take Susan home, and of course, Kenneth and Kathy stayed for a while. Giving Susan a peck on the cheek, Paul left her on her doorstep and saw her in, then took off back to the investigation and then at 2 am went home for an attempted rest. Why was this man murdered? He was just a dray driver named Soco Philips of good reputation and had been in Asheville since 1845, taking a room in a Boarding, unmarried, with no family, Socon was a bachelor who was trusted in town to faithfully and confidentially haul most anything for a reasonable fee. He was a Freewill Baptist, worshipping at the Baptist Church west of the Grove District there in town. He had been missing, and people were asking after him, but no one had expected foul play. Sometimes, he liked to go into the mountains to hunt and fish.

The South Carolina succession had started the ball of future fortune, good or bad, rolling, and the people became ambivalent about which way North Carolina would jump. But with a good 50% to 60% of the economy built on slavery, it was predictable that succession was secure. The investigators in Cherokee put dogs on the trail of Socon's grave, working from reverse to find the origination point of this murder. So, it was followed south and happened away from any proximity to the hidden gold. Someone had done some planting, but it had rained since the body had been moved, and the dogs were not as efficient at tracking as they had been in the past. The reservation dogs and trackers drew a blank. Paul, representing the Sheriff's dept, went back to Asheville and reported all this to the current Sheriff, Billy Wayne Weatherman, who was completing his second term as dully elected Sheriff of Buncombe County. Weatherman advised Paul to just go quiet on this murder for the time being, thinking that news of the perpetration would surface in about a week. In the meantime, the bank Socon had delayed from posting a $1500 reward for any leads pointing to how, where, and why he might have been murdered. Paul agreed with his boss and wrote down what he had learned in the last 48 hours. Indeed, work needed to be done tracking down Socon's last few work assignments.

The next day was a Friday, and Susan was busy at the bank all day, for Friday was payday all around for every business in Asheville and the surrounding farms, mines, and industry, of which there were a few, as a black smithy and tannery and large herbal pharmaceutical operation and indigo dying operation. The Asheville economy, based on these things, Agriculture and those mentioned, was reasonably diverse but not yet highly industrialized. There were livestock trading lots as drives moved cattle and sheep from the mountains to the southern coast of South Carolina, selling them off as they went. Yet now, with the thoughts of war coming, the prices of the stock on the hoof, cattle, sheep, and horses price points began to jump. Auctions became active, and stockyards burgeoned. The wealthy began to acquire more horses and cattle as the farmers thought they were being shrewd in selling some stock off for a higher price.

Now, Susan's father, Stanford Jackson, had the idea to sell future contracts on horses and cattle since he had the land and stock already and the means to breed more livestock and the slave base to do the work, grow the food, tend the stock and almost run a nursery so to speak. Standford sought to make the market regionally in livestock, thereby holding up the price and capitalizing his operations with a new profit center, the sale of futures. He enlisted his banking and real estate contacts and lawyers about town to help make a market in the future, and they were sold far and wide along the NC, SC, Florida, and New Orleans corridor. Almost traded like currency, Susan's bank assigned a check to manage the posting and issuance of the certificates, and though Susan did not handle them, she knew her Dad was the rainmaker, so to speak in this. Meantime, the Asheville Men's Club scene buzzed about this, and of course, at some level, everyone wanted the speculation.

As the secession of North Carolina became more than just an idea, the specter of it sobered the mountain community of Asheville, and hoarding of gold and supplies began to escalate unrelatedly but on a gradually increasing crescendo, and farmers began to prosper short term on their goods: produce wheat, corn, beans, and foodstuffs. Canning jars became scarce as they were obtained from up North New York and came through hardware stores, but there were no real chains. Pork hams were available, and a great cured country ham was a staple in the barn that people knew would keep and they could carry.

Kathy B. Generese' father, the grocer, got wagons from her boyfriend Kenneth and went north to buy goods that were hard to find but necessary, canning jars, salt, pepper, sugar, and other hardware. Also under the wagon tarps were hidden rifles, pistols, gunpowder and shots from dealers in NY and Chicago. They were sold at a premium, but Spencer figured he could double his money on these. Gone for a month, Mr. Generese had Kathy help mind the store while she was off time. When he did come home, he contacted Susan's father, Stanford Jackson, to find secure housing for the powder and arms to be metered out to the store for private transactions. Bunker style rooms were dug into the sides of hills in the country on the farms with heavily barred doors to store these items. And Stanford posted guards on them disguised as shepherds night and day.

The time for enlistments and conscription came in the Asheville area, and the young men, all fired up, signed up to go off for what they thought was a three- or four-week venture. And so, there were quick weddings, sweethearts wanting consummation of their love before the beaus went off to war. The sense in it was always questionable, but here in the hustle bustle of frantic activity, houses and churches held weddings and couples were gladdened before they could set up house-keeping and the ink dried on their wedding certificate. There wasn't much time. Half the Asheville units were to go to defend the west in Tennessee Mountains, there was the home guard, and then troops were sent to muster with Pettigrew and the North Carolina University boys to defend Richmond.

Susan worried that Paul would have to go, or decide to go, and likely he would; but there came a law enforcement officer's exemption except Paul deemed not to use it for he did not want to impugn his honor. So, on Tuesday night, December 1861, Paul came over to Susan's house to ask Stanford, then Susan, for her hand in marriage. He'd been saving for a ring for a very long time and had gotten Kenneth, Kathy's boyfriend, to order it from a jeweler in Atlanta. The ring was beautiful, with a ¾ carat center and ¼ carat baguettes, and so after going into the den with Mr. Jackson, he asked Mrs. Jackson to request Susan to come downstairs, and he knelt down and proposed right there in front of her mother and father. Susan was overwhelmed by some ambivalence and some joy and accepted, not really knowing what it meant for a future with the war and all. Stanford offered them a house to rent, and the wedding was set for two weeks; hence, Susan's mother, Joan, characteristically hugged Paul and Susan and went upstairs to cry. Paul and Susan decided to go for a buggy ride and out to supper to celebrate. It was a beautiful night, and it was not too cold. The street to the tavern restaurant was decorated modestly but tastefully for Christmas. Susan snuggled up close to Paul, and since they had dated for a long time, it felt right. Susan just did not want to lose him to the war which was on. Would be, but looks like they would have settled that first beforehand. No one questioned Paul's courage as a deputy sheriff, for he had seen law enforcement combat with criminals before. But this thing of a young man staying when others left; how it looked, how it felt, how it would be, Paul would have to live with all his life. The problem is that the siren song of the adventure and glory of war turns immediately to the gore and suffering of war as the first shot is fired. War is somewhat like a hypnotic medusa that attacks you and then strikes you with a lethal poison that kills. Walking into cannon fire would take courage, yes, but it is senseless on almost all counts, especially if you have a life to live. Yet the dedication to defense of hearth and home is so strong, the sound of the drums, the uniforms, the marching, the "cause" whatever it might be hypnotizes the male human for some reason, seemingly no other reason than to thin their population. Phrases to encourage enlistment would be bandied around; Preserve the home, send the yanks packing, later wars would call, first to fight, and so on. And so, amidst all this banter, static and true propaganda, Paul would have to make a decision that would affect him, Susan and unbeknownst to them, his newly conceived son.

Lawyer Johnson met Bank President Webster the following week at an out of the way tavern in up toward Waynesville. As a disguise, they wore farm working clothes instead of their everyday suits. This place was in a little house where lunch was served and day drinking was all day and into the night and it was a little rough around the edges for townsfolk but out of the way nonetheless, Lawyer Johnson greeted Bank President Webster over a beer in glasses and they pondered their next move.

One issue they were concerned about was the war and how it would affect the mortgages the bank owned and the string of rentals these men owned together in a corporation named New Vista Holdings. If the heads of families marched off to war and off their jobs, who was going to support the households to pay rents? This seemed obviously troublesome. The next question was, if they got their rent or a portion thereof, would it be paid in gold, U.S Currency or the new North Carolina or Confederate Script? The men pondered this and decided it was time to sell New Vista Holdings for a striking price they agreed upon in gold. They decided that they would discount the price a full 25% and market the property up north so that if they got buyers' interest, they could sell for gold. A northern buyer might think that he was getting the property on the cheap and that after the war, he could make a profit when real estate values presumably would go up. Banker Webster was to contact a Northern Bank to arrange financing for the buyer,, if any, and the plan was hatched to liquidate New Vista and to get the telegrams out today, marketing as the corporation and not typing it to them personally. The men decided to market the property regionally from Chicago East and Southward to Florida. Surely, there might be a speculator somewhere who had assets to invest in. The gentlemen tipped the waiters a dime apiece and went their separate ways.

Meantime, Deputy Sheriff Paul Edgars, and Sheriff Billy Wayne Weatherman met in the Sheriff's office to discuss the continuing investigation into the wagon driver, Socon Philip's murder. Socon was well-liked in the city, and politically, the case needed a report of progress. On that very crass level, it was an excuse to get more attention as a matter of righteous justice, Socon's blood called out for retribution. As there was no witness, no weapon found, no struggle, no prints, but some inquiry or listening in the area which he was found might produce results if a farmer dressed under cover set of deputies could frequent the watering holes and restaurants and they might hear a brag or a lead. This was set up, but it was likely to be of no avail as the perpetrator, Cherokee Warrior Sewakahony, was long gone, visiting Cherokee Kim in Oklahoma. As he had no living family in the Soco region, the trail would remain relatively cold.

Many attended Socon's funeral, and he was put to rest in the Old Asheville Cemetery.

The next week mobilization for the war began and enlistment stations were set up around Asheville city and the region. It was active, and here, Paul, seeing the public enlistments, had to mentally work through whether he would enlist or stay with the Sheriff's Department. He was married now though he still did not know of his son on the way. This was causing sleepless nights for Paul, and Susan intuitively knew why, though she did not know she was yet pregnant. Paul did have family in the area, and they implored him to stay, but people were looking down on young men who would not enlist.

While all this mobilization was taking place, Susan, still at the bank, noticed that the withdrawals had started with the common folk wanting to cash out in gold. One Monday, in surveying the vaults, the coin bag pile inventory seemed to shrink. With secession, there was no central Federal Bank to order gold from, and the bank had just begun to get the Asheville, N. C. Confederate script currency delivered. This was as new currency, folks only trusted gold and no longer trusted greenbacks. Susan did not know what Banker Webster and Lawyer Johnson had done, but she innocently told Mr. Webster that they needed to open some more bags of gold coins. Tipped off now, Mr. Webster had to hatch a plan to contact another bank to buy more gold coins. The pressure was on. Webster was going to come up short at some point. He stayed late after work to pull the punk metal coinage out, put it in his buggy, took it home and buried it in the backyard garden spot. He figured that until the balanced shortage was discovered he had time to hatch a plan to find a scapegoat to transfer the blame; though he knew within his conscience that the responsibility would land upon him. This is as he knew: a crook is a crook, but the prewar circumstances were Webster's excuse. For the rich, wealth preservation seemed to always trump honesty. For now, it was a bookkeeping entry to adjust, yet the pressure on the bank to produce the gold coinage when customers wanted to cash out was becoming acute with demand due to the coming war.

The demand for horses by the newly organized confederate army was burgeoning and Kenneth Lee Othario, Kathy's boyfriend who ran the livery and drayage decided to take a quick trip out to Wyoming to contact a rancher who might be a source for horses. After several telegrams, Jeff Shrank promised to put some of his best mounts on a railcar to Asheville, and Kenneth wired an initial deposit by wire to the Shrank Ranch as Kenneth Lee did not have to actually go out west. Kenneth was hoping that Shrank would choose horses that would be presentable and saleable to the new military. But there was more to it, for Kenneth planned to sell to both sides, being the sly entrepreneur that he was. He could ship horses, prepurchase to the Army depot in Maryland prepurchase and let them worry about breaking them, and of course, some of the Shrank Ranch had pre broken.

Kathy's father, Spencer Generease, was busy trying to stock up the inventory of all the items in a country store while the North South rail lines were still running. Yet he was ambivalent about overstocking, for with the patriarchs out of the house and off to war, how would the people pay? His had to balance his optimism and greed against his anxiety that nawed him in the background. War. The talk of it was easy, but people, on average, didn't really know what was coming. The veterans knew. It would be blood, sweat, tears, hurt, death and depravation if it lasted. The idealistic young buck confederates thought it would be up and over in no time, an adventure and back home. This idealistic approach led young troopers to leave for service ill equipped in clothing, footwear, arms, ammunition, and food stuff. The background timing of these pressures is related to the events. Secession as South Carolina had seceded from the Union on December 20, 1860, and as war pressure mounted, the confederates of South Carolina fired on Fort Sumter on April 17, 1861. There was time to react and prepare between December 20, 1860, South Carolina's secession and May 20, 1864, when North Carolina would follow with secession. In reality, it was only six months, and this was the reason the banks and lawyers were moving their gold and, people were hoarding, and merchants were stocking up on staples that they were afraid would become scarce.When We look back at this time in Asheville and the Mountains, time was not on the side of the poor, the unprepared, the city folk with no capacity for food stuff nor keeping livestock compared to the country farmers who could provide food for their families.

Deputy Paul Edgars continued to check with his undercover deputies, who were hanging around Soco Gap and the Cherokee Reservation. They had not turned a positive lead, so the Sheriff had posted a reward for information regarding the murder of Socon Phillips. The reward was 2,000 in gold coins. The funding of the reward was a little suspect for the Sheriff's Department only held about $500 in gold, but as bait, the reward was presented, and the Sheriff said it was for information leading to the arrest and the conviction of the perpetrator of the murder of Socon Phillips. That is a tall order and so the Sheriff figured that the risk reward ratio was worth taking the chance.

The so-called shepherds guarding Spencer Generase and Stanford Jackson's arms in the potato holds on Stanford's land were on the joint payroll of Generase and Jackson and were actually paid in shares of the sheep they were tending. It was an easy job if you liked the outdoors, and food and shelter were provided, as well as some spending money and a break to go into town. A lot like Webster dr0vers, these guardian shepherds were. The mountain people could keep secrets when they were paid enough. The six months between the secession of South Carolina in December of 1860 and the secession of North Carolina in May 1861 were quietly frantic. Asheville was influential in legislative politics.

The law office of Johnson Wipple Taylor and Young was busy with land transfer fees and wills and quietly moving wealth and protecting their wealth with much discretion. Miss Fanny, who was a receptionist, typist and experienced Paralegal, worked prim and proper with a little hat on. Type, type, type, greet a person, check with an attorney. She did this all with coolness and aplomb. Very efficient and courteous. She was a favorite of the upscale clients quietly entering the unmarked law firm. But Miss Fanny knew everything. She had a folksy manner that hid a mind like a steel trap. The key was that she had discretion, the number one requirement of a law firm. You could not pull the wool over Miss Fanny's eyes.

In Oklahoma, on a day amid the reservation, Sewakahony camped in the desert and subsisted on odd jobs day to day. But he became seriously distracted by a beautiful 27-year-old Indian maiden who was a nurse in the tribal dispensary named Eshanawa, meaning wind blows hair across face. Eshanawa had beautiful long black hair and rare, beautiful features and the wind after blew a hair veil across her face, hence her name. Swakahony set his bonnet for her and asked her to a tribal social. As she was like most beauties and not spoken for because the young bucks were too shy to ask her out, this worked in Sewakahony's favor. He was tall and strong and good looking, so they made a striking couple. This relationship was likely to bloom. Everyone observing said so.

The Webster, Johnson partnerships in New Vista Holdings got an offer from a speculative banker in Chicago. It met their specifications and so the many deeds were prepared, and the gold was given to the law office, and the Banker and the Lawyer, again, had a fortune in gold to hide. It went into the safe for now. Miss Fanny, who prepared all the contracts, took mental note of the transaction for it was sizeable and would create much attention at the register of deeds office. These gentlemen, Webster, and Johnson got this property sold in April, just before South Carolina fired on Fort Sumpter and before North Carolina's secession, and to get the gold delivery before all this was typical rich man's luck.

Susan was sick on Monday morning, about the fourth month after the wedding. She sent Mr. Webster a note that she would not be in. Of course, he was not happy about it, as the bank was under pressure as has been said for the secession news. South Carolina had fired on Fort Sumter and North Carolina secession was right around the corner. After the morning sickness, Susan decided to visit Dr. McLandish, who had delivered her and was her close family doctor. They sang in the choir together. Upon examination with nurse Emily present, he held her hand and said congratulations. You are pregnant about three months along. Susan welled up tears, and emotions flooded her soul. Here we are with a war starting, and I'm bringing a child into this world at the start of it. What if Paul leaves and goes off to war? The doctor gave her some ginger for the nausea and prenatal vitamin potion and said he'd see her again in three weeks. He said he wanted her to eat well and walk some every day. Fresh air and sunshine. Susan hurried home and awaited her Deputy Sheriff husband Paul, to come home to share the news!

In typical fashion for the mountain news, like a new baby traveled fast. Nurse Emily, though she had worked with Dr. McLandish for many years, was a busy body and a good friend of Susan's mother, Joan Fontaine Jackson. Soon as Nurse Emily got off work, she made a bee line for Joan's house. So, Susan's mama got the news before Paul did. Emily and Joan talked and talked about planning showers and quilting bees and what the nursery might be. Boy or girl, it didn't matter, for it was Joan's first grandbaby. Joan could not wait for Stanford to get home to spread the news. Meantime Paul aa Sheriff's deputy remember was working between Asheville and the Soco area where Socon Phillip's body had been found. Paul decided to make door-to-door inquiries of farms close to the discovery sight because nothing was being heard by the undercover deputies, who had spent too much time for no results. Paul pulled them in and released them to get back to Asheville to be reassigned. They were most glad to get back home, one to his family and the other to his sweetheart. Paul spent the day on horseback riding between farms knocking on every door he could find within a five mile radius of Socon's discovery site. Of course, people were guarded with a uniformed officer knocking on their door. Yet Paul was friendly and told them of the reward for information and how they had no leads. Paul thought that at least he'd gotten the word out, and it was time to ride home. He would have to let the inquiring simmer, and hopefully, a break in the case would come. Before he left, he checked in with the tribal law enforcement officer to update them, and he headed home. Meantime, there was finishing up an Indian wedding ceremony in Oklahoma. Sewkahony had won the heart of the beautiful Indian maiden

Eshonawa and the tribe had thrown them a beautiful wedding. There was much joy on the reservation that afternoon. Drums and flutes were sounding into the evening and a feast was laid out like Sewakahony had never seen before. Tonight, his heart was full of love for Eshanawa, but something shadowed the joy. The knew the Great Spirit was not pleased with him for killing Socon Phillips and a little voice in the back of his mind warned him there would be a price to pay. He shook off the thought and looked at his beautiful bride. Round they danced, for the night was young. And her hair blew across her beautiful face.

Paul's spurs sang as he stepped up on the porch of home and Susan heard the ring of it and ran to the door. As Paul came in, Susan grabbed him, hugged him and kissed him all over his face. Paul loved the affection but was a little taken aback. "It's good to be missed," he said. But Susan kept hugging, kept kissing and said between kisses, "we are having a baby. I've been to the doctor, and it's true!" Paul reacted with joy. He began to return to kiss Suan all over the face, picked her up and swung her around. Paul was elated! He was going to be a dad! There was joy in Asheville and Cherokee Oklahoma tonight! And it settled Paul's mind. He would stay home and not go off to service at least until the baby came and he could see his first child. It was as Susan had hoped but was not intentional. "God must have had a hand in this!" Susan thought that, as she had fixed a fine supper, they sat down to it, and Paul was famished from the ride home.

Meantime, having heard of the reward that day, a Cher0kee woodsman and game tracker decided to start where they found Socon's body and try to backtrack evidence from there. His name was Jehe Whanee, meaning "walks a lot," for a tracker must do so. This tracker was good.

Ranger Jeff Shrank had just finished loading a railcar with some fine range horses for Kenneth, the drayage and livery man in Asheville. They were scheduled for delivery the following week at the Biltmore Asheville rail depot and Kenneth planned to hire some men to drive them out the Swannanoa River Road and up to town to the drayage fenced lots. These horses would be wild and rowdy but also a little dazed from the long railcar trip. Shrank had done a fine job picking this stock, and Kenneth was going to be pleased with what he got. Another shipment had gone up to Indiana, and it was a long journey, but Shrank and Kenneth found that the Union paid well for good, healthy stock.

As North Carolina hadn't quite seceded yet, this was profiting but not considered aiding the enemy at this point. These men were merely tying to make a good living off the circumstances while they could. Yet the war spirit would have told them famine and deprivation would come, it always does in war.

The North Carolina Bank auditor cabled banker Webster he would be coming for his annual audit in April. As Webster read the note, he was filled with dread. How was he to cover up the gold discrepancy between the vault and the books, and who could it be to blame? Webster told Susan to have the staff get ready for the audit, and she began going over the hand-posted debts and credits journals to see that they balanced, and she found a $585,000 discrepancy in an original entry and a connection. Yet she thought this was merely a mistake and changed it yet again. But she did not audit the vault because she had a hard time in her pregnancy bending over. This would lead to Susan's downfall, as Webster had decided to blame the discrepancy on her. It would be a posting discrepancy, not a vault one. Webster had to hope that the auditor would not audit the vault. Usually, he would if he brought help with him. If not, it was more of a cursory ledger audit. Webster determined that if he had to sacrifice Susan to save his own skin, he would. Money generally makes men sorry. Here was a perfect case. But maybe it wouldn't come to that.

Ms. Fannie got off work and headed to the library. She carried an armload of books to return. Yet, that was not the only reason she was motivated to go. For Ms. Fannie had found romance amongst the bookshelves. In one corner on one book row in the fiction section, she had found a note: "To Ms. Fannie, I think you are wonderful" and Ms. Fannie, playing into it left a note, "Thank you" Who could this be? So, the conversation started every Wednesday, and note by note, the communication built into a sweet conversation. Who was her mystery suitor? The answer would likely come as soon as he asked something of her.

The bank auditor came two hours early on the day he had indicated. Susan showed him into Mr. Webster, President and head of the bank. He had come alone. The auditor's name was Frank Gilmore. He asked for a desk, some coffee and the last two years' ledger. Beginning there he gleaned each entry and made his notes. If he asked a question, it went to Webster, not Susan. However, the posting was neat and efficient, not a man's writing. He took a break for lunch, and before Frank left, he marked his place and carefully closed the ledger book. He ate lunch alone at a diner close by, savoring a dessert of apple pie. Upon leaving, he tipped the waitress and, walked back into the bank and went straight to the teller line to do a cash drawer audit. Finding no irregularities, Mr. Gilmore went back to his ledgers and, upon two hours' time, ran across an entry of December 20th, 1860, a correcting journal entry taken $578,000 out of cash and transferred to an entry: it was noted as New Vista Holdings. Yet when he checked their account, they found not $578,000 nor a deposit as such but a wire receipt for closer to $5 million. This puzzle he made a close note of it. It was now 4:30pm, Auditor Gilmore bid Susan and Mr. Webster "Goodbye for now." And so, he left back to Raleigh, where he would go. Nothing was said to indicate a discrepancy at the moment.

Out in Oklahoma, Sewakahony began thinking about the hidden gold. He was married now, and Eshanawa was now in a family way. Sewakahony began to hatch a plan to get back to Cherokee, North Carolina, to pick up some gold. He decided to hop on a train East and quietly get to the treasure without anyone finding out he had come back. So, he hopped the Santa Fe East and transferred in Knoxville to a Southern RR train rolling right into Bryson City and hopped off before he got into town. Moving through the woods, he went West toward the Soco Gap and up into the Northern hills. He made time and stopped at a clear stream for water. Moving up toward the cave, he moved rocks until he found the bags of gold coinage. Sewakahony decided when he left the cave to go north up toward Erwin, Tennessee, to catch a train back West. So far, he had been able to dodge human interaction and to move through the woods quietly and without disturbing the wildlife. The only thing was, now, there was a fresh trail from the cave north. And Jehewhanee, the tracker, was quietly and systematically working on a line to the northwest, and it would be a day when he would come across the track lines North Sewakahony had made, even though he had worn soft sole moccasins.

True to form, the tracker came across the trail north, which he did not follow north, but backtracked south, where he came across the cave. He did not go in but turned west to continue back tracking to the outskirts of Bryson City terminating at the railroad track. So, tracker Jehewhanee knew at least from where the trail started. He headed back to Asheville to report to Deputy Paul.

Meantime, clickety clack, clickety clack, headed back west was Sewakohony and a goodly load of gold.

The bank auditor wrote in his report that things looked alright except for a huge correctly journal entry that needed a further look, with a team. Mr. Frank Gilmore had been at this audit job with the State for nigh of 25 years and had experience with intuition. After the first of the year, unannounced, he would be back to check this out. By that time, it would be a coincidence that Susan would be out on maternity leave. That would move to be her undoing as Webster would blame her for the vault shortage and the odd journal entry.

A member of the law firm of Johnson, Wipple, Taylor and Young, George Wipple had just gotten back from Raleigh, where he reported the succession bill submitted to the legislator within days, the bill passed, and telegrams heated the lines all over the state. The lights did not go out in Asheville that night, and people were in the street. Folks on the Jackson farm were opening up their storage hills for the guns and powder that had been stored. Fannie was writing her note to her imaginary writer. Susan had paint in her hair, and on her face, as she was painting her great grandma's crib for the baby; Spencer Generese was busy in his general store unpacking provisions from barrels he had stored in the basement warehouse. Paul Edgars was traversing the city, keeping the peace as the wartime revelers lit bonfires all around. Banker Webster worked late. With Susan absent, and he could move more gold. And yes, lawyer Johson was there to catch it in his safe.

Kenneth Lee Othario's livery and horse stock business was busy tonight and another train car loaded of horses was headed both to Asheville and Springfield Il. Two of these mounts would meet again on opposite sides at Antietam, a fight that really no one would win except blood and death. Kathy knocked on the door at Susan's house, and Susan answered it, brushing her hair back with a blow and a swipe. "I've come to help you paint, she said. In spite of all this, friends have to make a future." And make a future a future they did through the ensuring hardships and the pain, the mountains stood prevailing against the war winds and flame. The names are still evident in the mountains and Asheville, a hub in the wilderness, so to speak. And politicians still go there to gain recognition and respect. Somewhere on an old Indian trail up on the reservation in Soco is a treasure still left undiscovered, and in Oklahoma, there is a family on the reservation who runs a clinic for the people. The Sewaka-Eshamawa Clinic is in honor of the parents who founded it with their prosperity.

The sun sets remain beautiful over the blue ridge as the new generations come, the spirits of those gone before declaring: No more war, please, no more, please.

And it is said that the tracker still roams the woods looking for signs of the murder of Socon Phillips. He did till he died in the woods at 92.

Chapter 1

Paul Edgars, deputy sheriff of Buncombe County was waiting for his operative tracker in the now six-month-old Scon Philip's case at a little country store on the edge of the Cherokee Reservation near Soco Gap. The tracker showed up on foot, came in and sat down at the table with Paul, and after some pleasantries about family, reported that he had not worked the north trail yet as the winter had been hard and the snow deep. Also, there was sickness in his lodge, and he had to tend to his children. Paul said that it was understandable and expressed concern for the family and gave the tracker an envelope with Yankee bills totaling $500 to continue the hunt for a sign of the track of this murder. They both had a small meal for which the deputy paid and shook hands, Paul going to his horse, a firm quarter stallion named Lightning, and Tracker headed back walking. Duty done, Paul turned and spurred Lightning to Asheville at an easy trot. The day was fine. It was a clear day and not too blustering and though still in winter months breaking spring would come soon, and Paul knew too that his wife sweet Susan was going to have his baby. The war had cranked up, and men out of the mountains were split on which side they would fight. Not all in the Western NC Mountains were pro slavery yet many signed up and the others armed up as if for trouble. Paul had to be ready to quell an insurrection and tomorrow he was to meet a secure shipment at the depot of the confederate notes and bills that had been printed for the banks to replace the Yankee greenbacks. If counted, it was cash for the area banks that totaled 35 million dollars. This was a large assignment to guard and work with the banking commission allocation to divvy and deliver the cash to as many as five bank vaults throughout the region.

There would be a cutoff date, and the new currency would be introduced in the South, here in Asheville and throughout the mountains. Paul had thirteendeputies assigned and eight wagons to carry either the cash or armed guards, and he hoped against all hope that there would be no raid on the delivery. Finally got to the Sheriff's office and tied Lightning to the post after watering him and. Paul brushed the dust off his jacket and reported to the Sheriff, Billy Wayne Weatherman, who quizzed Paul on the preparation for the morrow. They talked about their strategy, and then Paul left and took Lightning to the livery to be fed, wiped down and, brushed and watered again. Paul decided to walk across the hill home and surprise Susan with a bouquet of flowers purchased from a black lady purveying flowers up the street on the way home. Paul was tired from the day's ride but excited about the baby coming, and he loved his Susan, who was radiant in her pregnancy and seemed to be really happy and doing well, according to Dr. McLandish.

Meantime, Tracker made the lodge at the reservation where his family abode and had supper. He rested up and began to gather trekking supplies to begin his hike early in the morning of the North trail. The weather seemed to be going to hold and be pleasant, and so for the next week, Tracker planned to be in the woods looking for any sign of transport of the killer of Socon Philips. Tracker could live on next to nothing in the wild. The water ran pure where he was going, and he ate cold rations so as not to raise suspicion amongst the farmers of the region, as they would surmise, mostly out of prejudice, that he might be a thief. So, sunrise came, and Tracker set off quietly with his tracking dog named Skip. This dog was part German shepherd and part border collie, with the white, black and brown in all the right places and proportions.

Skip had a good nose, and Tracker never needed a leash for him, though he had made a collar for him and engraved his name in the leather. They had been together for nigh on 7 years, and Skip's nose was as good as there existed in the Western Mountain Region of the Carolinas and Virginia. Off into the morning mountain for they walked, into the mystery of the murder of Socon Philips.

Deputy Paul had been up since three am pacing and worrying about the 35-million-dollar shipment that was headed his way. He got to the depot an early two hours before the planned arrival, and as the wagons came up and the deputies showed up on time, he was gratified to have such good men. Now, all there was to do was wait for the wagon train to come into the station. Loaders would be ready to offload the money in crates disguised as country hams bound for the army. That, Paul thought, was a good touch since just wrapped bills would be too obvious. There were tarps to cover the crates, so this was a top-secret operation for a new confederacy, yet it was not known how the mountaineers would take to new paper money. Of course, Paul knew that people wanted gold coinage rather than paper in this war changed environment. Everything was set. Now, to continue awaiting the wagon train.

Tracker meanwhile began where over six months ago they had found Socon Philip's body. He headed North in the footpath that led from the valley up, up along the first escarpment of the smokies. It was an easy trail, but hard going as the trail arose from valley level to the higher mountains. There was no rush. Skipper, the dog, stayed with Tracker, and Tracker was looking left and right, far and near, for a sign, any sign that might lead to the killer of Socon Philips. He waited to find just a little mistake this killer might have made.

At Biltmore, the wagon train did come, and Deputy Paul and his cohorts sprang to action with stevedores offloading the crates marked "Country Hams" off the wagons and onto their wagons. As soon as the wagon was loaded, it was off to its assigned bank with a driver, a shotgun riding beside him and a deputy on each opposite corner. Up the hill from the depot the wagons pulled to the Main Banks uptown and then out the roads west and east and south of town to smaller banks and post offices along the way. Each stop got a package and a ham until that crate was empty, and this went on till dark. Then, the waggoneers gathered back at the central bank of Asheville to offload their overage, which would be delivered later by bank courier.

Up the trail, Tracker and Skip the dog trudged, and as they climbed, the creek got further down the ravine, of course, and Tracker slowly examined the water and surrounding rocks. They had lost sunlight in the dusky dark, so he and the dog settled in together aside the trail for the night. The next morning, after a cold breakfast of jerky, pemmican and water, Tracker and Skip began their inquiry along the trail. About noon on yet third day, when the sun was overhead, Tracker spied something white waving with the current out from under a rock in a little triangle wave. Was it anything? Was it a dead fish's fin? Oh no, I better check Tracker thought and so he started down the side of the mountain tree to tree, holding on and trying not to slide until he got to the creek bed. It took a minute for him to get oriented, and he walked along the west side of the creek until he saw a little bit of white coming out from under the rock, flagging with the current. Tracker looked all around, then lifted the rock, and there was a shirt! A crumpled-up shirt under that rock and one sleeve, the right one, was stained with sparkled blook stains fairly washed out by none but visible nonetheless in the bright sunlight. Tracker held the shirt up. It was of a wool liner flax makeup like trade goods might be made, white with bone buttons. You would see them often on the reservation. Tracker stuffed it in his pack after carefully wringing the shirt, all but the speckled sleeve out. Then Tracker squatted down and splashed his face and rested, he was trying to a make up his mind whether to walk the creek back until he could more easily climb the bank to the main trail. Made sense for him to do that, you know, and so he and Skipper picked their way down the rocky creek hoping not to lose their balance and fall in nor crack their heads in the process. As they moved purposefully and quietly, the fish darted into the water, and the crawfish scurried to hide. It was about four o'clock now and would be getting dark in an hour and a half. Tracker was thinking about trying to get back to the main trail up the bank so that they could hover up and curl up to fitfully sleep another night, so at the first opportunity, the dog and his master crossed the creek and fairly crawled up the steep bank to the main trail. It was an opportunity to be on the main trail and above the cold air coming off the water. That night, they lit a fire to warm, cooked a rasher of bacon and hard tack for supper, and went to sleep. Tracker had his arms wrapped around his backpack holding the shirt. The dog backed up against that, so Tracker and Skip were sleeping with a mere blanket over them in the Soco region of the Smoky Mountains, and the only witness to them was a hoot owl in a high red oak tree and a little beetle scurrying up the edge of the trail. As the woods fell silent and the stars came out, Tracker came to know what a measure of rest was to be as he had a start on finding the perpetrator of this murder.

Paul, the Deputy, was gratified that the delivery of Confederate currency had gone well. He figured that people weren't so sure about the new money and, hence, would not risk a robbery for what they thought was mere paper.

Paul, then, was waiting on three things; first was the birth of his new son or daughter, the second was the eventual retirement of Sheriff Billy Wayne Weatherman, and the third was that he was wondering how Tracker was doing in the north edge of the Smokey Mountains. Time would tell. The war had caused arguments in homes as families debated what happened with secession and the slavery issue. In the mountain region, some held slaves, and some didn't and, so sometimes a heated debate would occur with the family and the Sherrif's Department would have to intervene. As inflation of the cost of goods increased, it alone put pressure on the modest homesteads and the town's people who did not have land nor crops had to pay higher prices. Needless to say, hard scrabble living and a little liquor kept the city police and sheriff Department busy.

Meantime, out in Oklahoma, the perpetrator of the murder, Cherokee Warrior Sewakahony, now duly married and henceforth with a new son named Nevo Eva ("new start") and wife Eshawawa (wind blows hair across the face), were homesteading a place on the reservation. The gold that the warrior had brought back from his foray back to the scene of his crime, he had again had to hide their treasure, and this land was a little harder to find a good placement for treasure that would not be found by someone else. Also, he had come as a stranger and had married the most beautiful Indian maiden on the reservation. Many eyes were watching him. Who is this interloper? They said. So, the elders watched, but the jealous bucks watched closer. There were still old ties to the Blue Ridge of North Carolina, and possibly an emissary from the Oklahoma reservation might go back and do some checking. There was always that possibility.

The public notice went out in the papers from the banks that, on a certain date, the new Confederate money would go into circulation at face value. That did not mean that dollars, Yankee dollars, would be refused, but that the conversion over time to the new currency would be affected. In the mountains, the old timers who were savvy hoarded their gold, what little they had.

Tracker spent a good day moving back south on the trail. Skip dog trotted right out front of him about twenty feet or so. They were having a good time. Yet on the ridge above a little ways back, a denizen of the forest was tracking them too. It was a black panther. Paul, the deputy, spent the morning checking on equipment and his horse, then went into the office to check any new warrants that had come in. And he was awaiting news from the war, from the Sheriff, from Susan, his wife and awaited Tracker to find if he had any success.

The meeting of troops, many from the western part of North Carolina traveled by wagon & horses to Raleigh, where they mustered in with Pettigrew's troops and the volunteers from the University of North Carolina, and some were assigned to Johnston on the coast. Yet Pettigrew's troops went up to defend Richmond and combined with Lee's Army of North Virginia. There, they were assigned as needed to Trimble, AP Hill and others, and many of them would fight in every major battle that would come until the end.

Asheville was starved for true war news. Not rumor but **w**ar news. Paul and his friend Kenweth Othario, who dated Susan's friend Kathy Generase, needed news from the Army about the demand for horses, as the shipment was scheduled to arrive, half in Asheville and half in Springfield, Illinois. Though attempting to keep it secret, Kenweth was planning to sell horses to both sides. It was a straddle that he would regret in the future, for in Asheville, there were more people talking about his business than he was talking. "Tell a girlfriend, tell the world, the old saying goes, but here, that and the bank watched as the drafts cleared as to where the money was going. Track the money they did and so nothing was really confidential as the war heated up. Right now, it was in the gathering phase, then it would be in the posturing phase, and when it got hot and bloody, it would be in the winning phase and then would come the seeking and burying phase. The gatherings and posturing's had started the true hell of it was yet to come. But right now, what people wanted was news.

Kenweth Lee Othori0 who ran the livery and had ordered the horses to sell to the armies, had to have found out the procurement offices and what the confederacy would be willing to pay for good horses. He had a carpenter and a wheelmaker, holding them on the string, so to speak, working on a sample freight wagon, a troop carrier and a caisson for cannon service. These prototypes were made of good oak, and an interesting note on the troop carrier was that he had made the suspension and wheels extra heavy and the sides of oak four inches thick in four layers. It made the wagon heavy but was an attempt at armor for the sides of the wagon, which was not obvious, as metal would be from the outside. This, he hoped, would impress the procurement officer and fetch a premium price for each wagon, selling the durability as a feature, too. It all came down to capability and ability to turn a dollar. Of course, Kathy's father, Spencer Generase, needed livery vehicles and horses for his deliveries, and he had a nice, reasonable arrangement with Kenweth. Yes, there was uncertainty with the war, but it was in the gathering phase without the killing yet, and the south was optimistic, everyone except Veterans of the War of 1812 and Indian Wars. In a true war for a reason, usually, there was more blood than money left and the man making the money was the undertaker, who, by the way, was bidding on stands of timber to make his coffins from. It was going to be big business. Yes, the funeral business, for you see, the government would be bidding those contracts out, too. Indeed, there would be general inflation all around. Remember that Kathy's dad with the general store had preordered weaponry in pistols and rifles and ammo, and these had been stashed on Jackson's land in guarded bunkers. Now was close to the time profiteering on them, for during the euphoria of the gathering phase, here was inherently the equipping phase and after the first few battles with equipment loss and theft. The cooperators in this project were ready, awaiting the disasters; battles far off which would generate the need for a replacement gentlemen stood ready to help the highest bidder with quick delivery of replacement equipment and arms.

Stamford Jackson, Susan's Dad, a director of the Asheville Bank and a huge landowner of farms throughout the mountains, had his slaves; the ones that had not snuck off working on produce crops and staple crops, beef and hogs and poultry and had a distillery for spirit dink, "for medicinal purposes – only" as well as saw mills throughout the mountains harvesting timber for railroad ties, the wagons needing built and beams for earthworks, and of course ladders and for replacement on buildings and such. Stamford's holdings were vast, and his business was vertically integrated in many facets, but all were based on slave labor. Stamford's intent was to be a major supplier of goods for the confederacy, and since he held slaves, he did not seek to track both ways with the Yankee. Remember that he and the bank president, Eunicile Webser, where friends as Stamford was on the bank board, so he knew that the Confederate dollars had come in and when the date of conversion was. In the meantime, he sought to convert most of his cash accounts to gold, which was the remainder he had and converted just before the secession. So, one day, he went to the bank and asked Mr. Webster to order up the value of his accounts in gold. And here was the tipoff. Mr. Webster told him that they would have to order gold from Raleigh, that they were some short of matching his accounts and that it might take a matter of weeks to get a shipment in. A little bell went off in Stamford's head. He said nothing, for he could check in with Susan, his daughter who worked for the bank.

Susan, in the meantime, was feeling very much with the child. She had been working still in her pregnancy, but it had now gotten awkward as she was near to term, and her ankles were swelling from sitting at her desk, and she could not get down into the file cabinets nor climb any filing ladders to get records. Susan would blow and blow in heavy breathing and discomfort, much less having to visit the lavatory sometimes three times in an hour and a half. Susan was ready to have this baby. So was Paul. It was first on his mind.

One day, three weeks hence, Paul was in the Sheriff's office working but saw Tracker walking by, who slowed by the window and waved. That was the signal to meet him at the diner over at Soco the next day. Tracker did not want to go into the Sheriff's office as the bar cages made him nervous.

The next morning, Paul kissed Susan, got dressed, grabbed a biscuit, saddled his horse and headed to rendezvous with Tracker at a little nondescript diner on the roadway. Since the diner was on the Reservation, they served Indians as well as whites, but not coloreds nor Chinese. It's just the way things were at the time. Paul headed west at a slow trot. He had plenty of time, and as he headed across West Asheville and on toward the Smoky Mountains, he practiced being hyper observant, looking for signs of trouble, you know, the war and all. And he actually stopped to look up under some of the bridges just to identify sabotage if it was happening. Paul carried a revolver of the time and a rifle and had a knife in his belt, though the badge on his chest and his long-time experience and official manner carried him a long way with the public. It did not hurt him to have married Susan, who was a nice central figure at the bank and had many customers, both large and small. As they attended, when he could, the First Baptist Church of Asheville with many members, and the fact that when Sheriff Billy Wayne Weatherman, his boss, retired, Paul anticipated getting his endorsement in his run for Sheriff... if the war did not conscript him first. So, things were reasonably positive, assuming the baby came ok, and that Tracker had something. He must, Paul thought otherwise he would not have walked plumb to Asheville to signal him. At the same time, Tracker and Skip headed east through the valley to get to the main road up Soco Gap, where the diner was located. He timed his leaving and his walk to arrive just as Paul arrived, too. He would show Paul the evidence outside before they went in and give it directly to Paul. Make of it what they could, and yes, there was a mark on the corner of the shirttail. It was a Cherokee mark. But they knew not yet whose mark it was.

It was the following Thursday when the baby came, Susan struggled, but after 12 hours' of labor, Dr. McLandish delivered an eight-pound baby boy to be named Bradley Jackson Edgars. He had blonde hair and blue eyes and was hungry from the start. Paul picked him up and his heart melted in emotion, the grown man tearing up. He was a father, now the real thing. Paul and Susan were ecstatic, and so were Stamford and Joan Jackson. It would be a day to remember for things would be changed in time. Susan's friend Kathy arrived to help take care of the baby, but she was as foolish as the parents and grandparents about little Bradley. There was joy in the morning in the Edgar's house .

Deputy Paul had asked Tracker to inquire within the reservation about the mark on the corner of the shirt. Tracker went lodge to lodge inquiring about the women who might have seen that mark. They said that it seemed no one was using it now, and they had not seen it doing laundry nor hanging on a line but said they would keep an eye out for it and contact Tracker if it showed up on anything.

Tracker took a rest, and then, with Skipper, the dog decided to go up the trail where he found the shirt north, looking for more signs. This would be a six-day journey, and this time, he packed a little heavier and quietly left the village, vectoring to cross the trail at an angle, cutting off some miles of the ground he had already covered. There were all kinds of trails vectoring and crisscrossing the reservation, so it was not hard to find one that would work to Tracker's advantage.

Meantime, the war between the states heated up, with the first battles being Manassas, Philippi, and Shiloh, and the losses began to come in. There was no scarcity yet. However, the north had quit moving some goods south because the rail lines had been taken for moving armies and armaments.

Kenneth Otario's investment in horses to sell both the confederacy and the union was becoming an anxious endeavor as there had not been enough battle yet to have expended horses to create the demand that Kenneth expected. Meantime, while he waited for telegrams from the procurement officers of both sides, the horses were eating. And eating and eating. Besides, in Springfield, Illinois, Kenneth had livery fees for storage piling up. Hence that batch he proposed to sell to the public at a reasonable price. He telegraphed his livery there to place ads in the paper for the sale, and he would test the market for horses with the northern public. Never mind that they were half broken and still a little wild.

There in Asheville, Kenneth cabled the procurement officer for the confederacy district in the northeast of Virginia who was Adolphus Mabry, slashing the price on this first batch of horses to establish a supply line. He awaited the answers to both contacts and then sought to sell some of these horses locally/regionally, too. A little time would tell how this endeavor worked out for him. However, Kenneth was enterprising, and the success generally came to those who worked for it. The livery stable was busy and could carry the feeding of the horses. The next time he saw Stamford Jackson, he would inquire of him first if he needed horses in his farming or logging and lumbering business, and second, if not, he would lease some pastureland to him for a time. That, Kenneth thought, might make a good solution to his quandary. In the meantime, the war in the east ground on, mostly in Virginia, with the suffrage there and the price being paid by the men and women of many confederate states. So far, Asheville had been spared except for goods that had been coming from the north.

The greatest impact on Asheville and the surrounding farms was the lack of men to oversee the deputy business chasing down altercation between slave owners and their slaves or runaways. This was a distraction for Paul, who was now a new father and busy deputy with an influx of wartime fraud and penny thievery.

Althewhile Tracker had vectored onto the northern trail, just above where he had stopped last time. He and dog Skipper hiked the trail, then back tracked and came up the creek, looking for more signs. They worked for days, making light camp and studying every bit of the trail and Creekside. Up and down, up and down. The work was tedious and hard. There was, of course, evidence of Indians hunting this land: old campfire rings and a few spent arrows. On the eighth day, alongside the main trail, he found a stick sticking up and did a little digging. There was a bloody rag, or a rag with blood dried upon it like it had been used to clean a knife or tomahawk or other weapon. "Why not burn that rag?" he thought, yet he remembered that the murderer did not want to make fire to signal his whereabouts. Tracker tucked the rag in this possible bag and marked the spot off the trail with a stack of rocks. It was as if the ground was shouting out to tell him of the hideous crime.

The next morning, Tracker and Dog Skipper headed north again. They combed the trail and creek sides again. Nothing came up until the next day, and they found where a man had left the trail, headed northeast. They followed and eventually came to a railroad cut through the mountain gap. The rails ran east to west, and so Tracker figured that the murderer hopped a train, but which way, he did not know. Tracker turned and headed for home. There wasn't much else to do at that time. He would report his findings to Deputy Sheriff Paul. The little dog panted by his side.

<hr>

Chapter 2

Kathy Generase, whose father owned the largest general store in Asheville, really enjoyed looking after Susan and Paul's son, baby Bradley Jackson Edgars. When Susan was coming off the time to go back to work, Kathy agreed to keep Bradley for almost no fee, something, but a very modest one. Kathy came to the house each day early and would leave when Susan came home. Since Kathy had helped her father in the general store, she arranged to come in and work from 6 till 8 when the store closed. Her dad, Spencer Generase, agreed with this arrangement, for he was at the store most all the time. Six months into the war, there were some scarcities of goods that had come from the north, but since Asheville was agricultural in the surrounding area, the store could get foodstuffs. It was largely hardware and metal goods that were a little harder to get now. Yet Spencer had, over a long time, made contacts to get what he needed, even if he paid a premium for wholesale price. Susan's mother, Joan Fontain Jackson, was foolish as all grandmothers about the baby and would visit about every other day, giving advice and making clothes for Brad in the New Orleans style. Meantime, Grandfather Stanford was overseeing his many holdings and doings wartime trading on the side, selling guns, and lumber, foodstuffs shipped by wagons from Kenneth's livery into Virginia as far as Richmond by skirting the border and moving at night then up to Richmond as the way to Richmond was kept clean by confederate troops. Some shipments got waylaid by roving bands, but for the most part, Stamford found safety in numbers of three to six wagons, each with a driver and rider. In Asheville, the older middle-aged men had not gone off to fight, but they wanted to contribute to the war effort and make some money, too. Here, driving and guarding these wagons satisfied both goals and also provided a sense of adventure for these men.

Stamf0rd Jackson and Kenneth Lee Othario had come up with a way to shield the wagon loads with triple sides of oak and in particular, the sides of the driver's bench on the side above the head height of the driver and rider so that it would be hard to get a bullet into them except a head-on angle. They were protected across their back with a panel of the triple oak. This was a new concept in a camouflaged armed wagon and worked reasonably well and gave both driver and guard confidence in their protection. Of course, the horses were still vulnerable, and this could not be helped. This was the weak spot in the armor of the wagons.

Yet Stamford Jackson sent wagons out after harvest time of all forms of produce, processed meat and patent medicines made in the mountains by mountain grannies. These things were much appreciated by the Confederate army and Stamford was no philanthropist. He charged as much as the market would bear and preferred to get paid in gold if he could get it.

In Oklahoma, the Indian Warrior and murderer, Sewakahony, was thriving on the reservation with his wife, Eshamawa and little son, Neoeva. Sewakahony managed to buy some feeder's calves, and they were small, but he and his wife bottle-fed the calves from a couple of milk cows till he could graze them on open reservation land for gaining weight for the market. This was slow, but certain money if the cattle did not get rustled. He decided to brand them with his mark, SM, for smoking mountain in remembrance of the Great Smokies back home. He had used that mark for his identification before. The stylized mark was in Cherokee, but you could see the meaning in the mark. Of course, around their cabin, Sewakahony and Eshamawa had some horses, a bro0d mare and two stallions and a colt, chickens, hogs, goats and new calves. There were many fences on the spread. They had to pay dearly for the lumber to make them, for there was no forest where their cabin was set. Yet to get there, so many trips with the wagon over a period of months were necessary to collect enough posts for this fencing. The Elders, sitting, watched all this work and asked themselves, who is this brave, come from the east? We must find out more about him. So, in council on the fifth day of April 1862, they commissioned one of their brave lieutenants, so to speak, to head east with ears for which to hear who the Sewahony was and more about him. Instead of hopping the train, the tribal elders collected enough for a ticket. This brave would have to earn his way back.

The non-descript law firm of Johnson Taylor and Young continued to prosper, what with the regular legal work and filing quitclaim deeds against properties of the men who had left their lands and families to go soldering, plus the purchase and sale of contraband goods and cash for gold, that is confederate cash for gold schemes, the lawyer made a confidential tidy sum which in gold, they held in their vaults and the confederate money they used their connections to convert either to gold or to property, Commercial property if they could, or farm timberland. They even traveled east to the coast to purchase with Confederate money loblolly's forests, set up sawmills and reach sites for naval stores, selling these both to the South and North through agents in the South and north. Of course, the work was done by an overseer and slave laborers. These were true assets bought with Confederate money but sold for gold.

Quietly, the lawyers bought ironworks. Basically, it was a forge on the outskirts of Boone, and they procured from Brittain a mold for a modest cannon to forge and pour. It was done in two pours and band forged. These were bought, of course, with the Confederate money and sold for gold to the confederate government. The cannons proved useful, more as mortars with a lighter charge of powder since the barrels were poured into two pieces. Yet they were deadly with grapeshot at reasonably short range.

As the law firm quietly prospered, Miss Fanny, the receptionist, was privy to all this within reason, and yet she maintained loyalty and said not a word. And from time to time she was allowed to buy in on a venture. Everyone thought when the war breaks out, there will still be money to be made. Miss Fanny had simple needs and simple pleasures. She just wanted to be participative and have a little nest egg, war or not.

George Whipple, the Asheville Bank president, dropped by Susan Jackson Edgar's home to pay a visit and to inquire as to if and when Susan would come back full-time. Susan had it arranged with Kathy Generase to keep the baby from coming in half a day. The reason Mr. Whipple wanted her to work more was because State Auditor Frank Gilmore was coming back for a follow-up, and he was going to need her help. Unbeknownst to Susan, Mr. Whiple knew his bank was shorn up with faulty assets, and the gold had been moved. He needed a scapegoat. Susan was the first obvious one. This would be an awkward needle to thread as Stanford Jackson, Susan's father, was on the Bank Board. It also made his plan plausible. Susan agreed to come in full days, three days a week. As she was capable, trained, and easy on the eyes, it was good for Mr. Whipple. It might later prove Susan a challenge.

On an early morning, Paul Edgars was in his office when a visitor came in to see him. It was John Philips, Socon Philips' brother. Paul had not seen him since the funeral, so he greeted him, and they sat down. John was in good stead, but he wanted to know how the murder case of his brother was going and if there had been a breakthrough or any information or if he could be of any help. Paul told him of some clues in general terms and that he was waiting for his informers to get back to him, who would shortly, and he would come by John's place and show him what he had found. John left amicably, and Paul was gratified that he was not upset about the lag in justice here. Paul pulled the shirt out again and looked it over. The blood spatters were there, and in the corner of the shirttail, he had not seen it before, it was inverted with wavey lines above it. Very small. Mumm, he thought, I need to head over to the Soco and see what might be known about that. As it was early morning, he got some provisions and headed out toward Soco and the reservation. Paul took his time just plodding along, but once on the reservation, he began really looking for signs. Sign of the inverted V with the wavey lines. He did not know what it might mean. Was it the owner of the shirt, the maker of the shirt or merely a laundry mark? Paul did not know but looked for that mark everywhere. He stopped by the reservation law enforcement office, which was really an abode hut. He was going to take the shirt in and then thought better of it because they might want to seize it since the murder happened on the reservation and they might have rights to custody. So, Paul wrote a drawing of the inverted V and wavy lines on a piece of paper and asked if they knew anything about that mark. The attendant referred to the officer in charge, who looked down at the paper and then into Paul's eyes. He said nothing much, but Paul knew that the man was familiar with the mark and was not letting on about it.

Actually, the mark standing for wind over the mountain was a clan sign, and the officer knew not only what it was but was a member of that very clan, or large family, so to speak. This would present Paul with a problem at some point, but not now, as the deputy officer of the tribal enforcement's home was Hosekahony and would be a direct cousin to the murderer, Sewakohony. Paul thanked the man and continued on to the diner, where he and the tracker would generally meet and break bread together. Once there, Paul tethered his horse and went inside for coffee and a piece of pie. He asked the proprietor to look at his paper showing the inverted V and asked him, "what's this?" and he replied, this is a clan symbol, yet I don't recognize it as active in the tribal government recognition now. It must be ancient, not in regular use. This seemed odd to Paul, but he had read of clans in Ireland and the Mideast of yore, which dated back to the Middle Ages. In thinking about this, Paul discerned that this might be an underground Cherokee clan of resistance from an old-line family. Paul decided to venture further into the reservation to check to see if there might be such carvings or paintings or totems showing the inverted V or wavey lined sign or rune or whatever. He also wanted to visit one of the tribal elders, who was a friend of his father's who might have an idea about the sign. So, looking along several trails and in the market, Paul did not see any sign resembling the inverted V. He called upon his family friend, Cherokee Elder Running Wolf, who was 83 winters old and had befriended Paul's father while hunting in the mountains and who had gotten caught in a snow storm and needed shelter and Running Wolf took him in. They became friends, so Paul was welcome in Running Wolf's lodge, and they kept close touch. After many pleasantries and talks, Paul produced his paper showing the inverted V and asked Running Wolf about it. Running

Wolf pondered, then stepped back into his bedroom, and Paul could hear him rummaging around. Running Wolf came out with a hidden scroll that looked very old. He unrolled it on the kitchen table. It was marked with many signs. Yet in green on the leather was the mark V^ with wavey lines over it. And Running Wolf explained that its name was Clouds over the Mountain. He said it was an ancient clan that was not recognized now because it was a dark clan known for clandestine operations which had been outlawed by the tribe for centuries. Running Wolf had acquired this scroll hide from his father, who got it from his great-grandfather, and it dated almost from historical obscenity.

Paul did not tip his hand by telling Running Wolf of his find of the shirt and the sign on it. Instead, he invited Running Wolf to the baptism of his new little son, which was held Sunday week for Jackson Edgars, and asked Running Wolf to decide a Cherokee brother's name so that he could be smudged after the baptism. So here, Running Wolf picked up his long pipe and said ceremoniously, "Let's ask the Great Spirit while we smoke on it."

Lighting the pipe, Paul smelled the strong tobacco, and Running Wolf took a long pull and then passed the pipe to Paul, who took a very short pull but held the pipe in reverence. Running Wolf closed his eyes, and then it seemed a long time, as he rested, breathing very lightly, eyes closed and finally raised his eyes and put his hands in the air and announced that the baby's Cherokee name Snows Friend, for he had met his grandfather in the snow and they had become last friends, Paul greatly agreed. They both took another draw on the pipe, and then Running Wolf cleared it and gently set it aside. To celebrate the decision, Running Wolf picked up a ceremonial drum cantation, which lasted fifteen minutes. And then, they rested. As it was getting darky dark, Running Wolf asked Paul to stay the night after supper. Good courtesy as Paul was like family demanded Paul stay, so he agreed. Running Wolf's wife began to work on the supper while Paul stoked the stove and RunningWolf fetched water. There would be feasting and good talk tonight in the simple Cherokee lodge on the Soco.

Paul excused himself to tend his horse and then walked around the village while awaiting dinnertime. Running Wolf walked with him as they discussed the investigation of the murder and old times, and

Running Wolfe gave pointed directions for improvements that had been made on his small farm. One major improvement was a new barn that held room for livestock and had a birthing station and a milking section as well as a loft for hay storage and, in one corner, a small still which Running Wolf had found in his ramblings about the mountains. It was not operational, though he might claim it was for tribal medicine.

From Oklahoma, the tribal elder's emissary who had been appointed to investigate Sewakahony had entered Georgia and was slowly traveling up the roadways of the forest now actually travel paths, centuries-old, toward the 50-mile outskirt of the reservation. There, he would begin to quietly make inquiries of his kith and kin. Each place of inquiry, he would introduce himself to a person in charge and show papers lending his credential authorization for the Elders' inquiry. It stated that this was tribal business and much confidential and requested hospitality for their emissary.

CHAPTER 3

Paul Eggerton, Sheriff's Deputy, was visiting Running Wolf on the reservation and had been invited to supper. Upon completion of a walk, he returned to Running Wolf's lodge and washed up for supper. The women had been cooking while Paul had been on his walk. As the family gathered round, Running Wolf reached out his hands and led a prayer, and then the family sat down at a long table. Paul looked forward to eating deer tenderloin, wild turkey, sweet potatoes, corn and green beans. For dessert, there were baked apples. To drink, there was a pink tea made from Sumac and sweetened with honey. After a formal introduction, everyone was served. Running Wolf asked each child what he or she had learned that day. It was a tradition of his. Each one, in turn, answered with their vocal contribution to the subject. Finally, Running Wolf spoke of how he had a good day showing Paul around, and Paul told him what he had learned while walking around the reservation. As the women cleared the table, the children begged Paul to tell them a story. This has been a tradition ever since Paul visited Running Wolf. The children knew that Paul was their dad's friend, and they loved his stories, which were sometimes about chasing crooks or about his little baby son, Bradley. Sometimes, Paul would tell of the city of Asheville, and the children were spellbound, for they had never traveled outside the reservation. Paul talked about breaking horses, shooting rifles, ghost stories of Asheville and about things the children knew about, hunting, fishing and games. Of course, Paul went into many antics while telling these stories, and the children laughed gleefully. After the stories, it was time for the children to do a few chores, then come in, wash up and prepare for bed. Paul and Running Wolf smoked and talked of old times. Then as the women got their children bedded down, the men sought their beds, and the fire died down, and there was sleep in the camp.

During the night, everyone rested as they had full bellies and good humor and no worries to trouble them, at least for now. The next morning came early to Paul, but he wanted to get an early start back to his place in Asheville, so he was saddled up by 6:00 after profuse thank you' s all around and rode back east toward Asheville at an easy going pace. Paul had learned what he had come for and also many other things about his adopted family and friends. It was interesting to Paul to see how they lived and to see how they died. Life on the reservation could not be taken for granted. Paul was also thankful for Running Wolf's friendship.

Paul rode straight home to check on Susan and Brad. Paul found Susan and Bradley fine, but the woodpile was a little shy, so that he knew he would have to chop some wood in the evening. Turns out that Susan had given some of their wood to a woman who had already lost her husband in an early battle in and around Greensboro, and so, as a widow, it was hard to get the outside chores done if you did not have young men to help in the family.

Paul checked in with the acting Sheriff and made his report. Acting Sherrif, Billy Wayne Weatherman, acknowledged that he had heard of an assassination clan of old times among the Cherokee, though he had not heard anything about it lately, as in the time he's been sheriff for the last fifteen years. It was more legend, that he had heard amongst frequenters of the reservation and heard bar stories told late into the night. It would be yet another week before Paul's next meeting with Tracker, but Paul had local enforcement to work and some time to make up with Susan and little son Bradley.

Meanwhile, the men who enlisted with the confederacy had

mustered in with Pettigrew's boys from the University of North Carolina and went up to defend Richmond. Some went to the coast under General Johnston to defend Wilmington. Battles began to ensue, and the casualty lists were posted at city hall. Wives checked the lists every day. Written copies were posted at the churches in rural areas for those who could not get to town. Bad times were coming. It was easy to talk of war, winning a war, but to prosecute a war was another thing. The hell of it all is that families had to go and retrieve the bodies of the dead. First, they had to find them. Now, Kenneth Lee Othario's horse project looked a little better as both sides lost their poor horses to gunfire, cannonade and exhaustion. There became a market of demand for horses, and though gradual, a market for both the blue and grey for replacements appeared. Kenneth made his contacts on both sides. He had bought horse inventory early and had been feeding them, so he needed to get a good price for them, which was going to be a challenge. Actually getting paid was going to be a challenge, too. Yet Kenneth was game, and he made his contacts, and contacts and prepared for delivery.

The Emissary from Oklahoma was now making informal inquiries around the edges of the reservation as to Sewakahony and if he had any kin in the area. Of what clan he might be in, how he was living before he left, and if anyone had an idea about why he might have left suddenly. Eventually, though, the Emissary needed to approach the elders before the rumor got back to them that there was a stranger asking around. So, the Emissary made his way straight with his credentials to the Chief's administrative lodge to introduce himself and present his papers from the Oklahoma Tribal elders. He did get an audience with the chief after waiting three days. And so Manakee, "runs so far," met Santeela, great chief of the Cherokee, presented his credentials and posed his questions about Sewakahony. The Chief, Santeela, said he would make inquiries of the elders and would summon Manakee in three days. In the meantime, he offered him a quest lodge to stay in and offered supper with the elders that night. Manakee was grateful, for he had journeyed long and hard. He found the lodge accommodations fine and rested, then got cleaned up to meet the elders that night.

In Asheville township, Kathy's father, Spencer Generese, who owned the large country store in Asheville, readied himself for a trip selling guns to the confederacy. Bringing rifles out of hiding, powder and shot, he had previously ordered a wagon built through Kathy's boyfriend, the livery stable owner, Kenneth Lee Othario. This was a sturdy freight wagon with canvas cover and a double floorboard in order to hide the guns. He loaded the wagon with barrels of salt pork and dry goods to carry and sell to the Confederacy, as well as the guns. The wagon had a sleeping quarter just back of the protected bench driver's seat, and it was built for safe travel on roads across the state. Spencer planned to leave in the middle of the night to get down the mountain before dawn, and Kathy was going to mind the store while he was gone. Kenneth was headed to Morganton, descending down the steep Black Mountain range. As the sun came up, he was on that slope, and he was going to Statesville, Winston, Greensboro and Raleigh to sell goods, guns and powder to the Confederate units deploying off to war. He sought to bring back hardware and much-needed seasonal supplies such as salt and sugar used seasonally for baking and preserving pork and beef, which were seasonal coming up when falling hog killings began. He also wanted to bring home bolts of cloth for the women who sewed and whale oil for lamps and other necessities to stock his store. So, Kenneth lit out easy, following the road down the mountain through the Swannanoa gap and over, brake holding back for the far mile descent down the steep Black Mountain range. As the sun came up, he was on that slope, and he was glad for more light, which allowed him to slowly pick his way down the mountain.

Deputy Sheriff Paul Eggerton sought to talk with his tracker again and to get him tracking north further, looking for signs of Socon Philip's murderer. He settled up and rode toward the Soco, looking to find a tracker at a tavern watering hole he frequented. It took Paul two days to find him, having imposed on Running Wolf's hospitality once again. It was really not an imposition for Running Wolf to count Paul as family, and he had a standing invitation for when he was in the area. Paul and Tracker sat and talked about what each knew: Of the evidence of the shirt, the blood stains on the shirt, and the wind over the mountain clan sign evidence there. Paul told Tracker to be judiciously careful in his inquiries and to be observant at all times because this supposedly extinct clan, known for assassination for hire, must not be extinct anymore. Who was involved, Paul or Tracker, did not know. Paul asked Tracker to quietly listen and look for any sign of the clan as he investigated the murder of Socon Philips. Paul paid Tracker for needed supplies for an extended search and bid his adieu. He needed to get home after two days gone. Paul rode a little more quickly away this time, trying to beat sundown home. He needed to catch up with his wife, Susan, and little son, Bradley.

Susan had a hard day and was ready to leave the bank early that afternoon. Brad had kept her up half the night, and bank president Eunicile Webster had been calling her to his office frantically all day as he had gotten a telegram that the bank auditor, Frank Gilmore, was coming back to check assets, physical assets this time. It had President Webster pacing, though Susan could not fathom any reason why,. The bags were in the vault as always. Susan knew of nothing awry.

Miss Fanny, secretary and receptionist for Johnson, Wipple, Taylor and Young, caught up on her work and had dozed off at her desk for a moment when at 1:30, a rap rap rapping on the door startled her and woke her up. She took a moment, then got up and answered the door, straightening her little hat as she walked over to do so. Fanny pulled the door open, and there was bank president Eunicile Webster wringing his hands in a pure state of nervous anxiety. He asked to see the lawyers, all of them in private, and Fanny escorted Mr. Webster to the conference room and, sat him down and brought him a cold sarsaparilla and a small cake. She bid him to relax and said that she would get the lawyers. Fanny left the conference room open and went office to office, bidding for each lawyer to come. Each looked up and did come, though this was an unusual event, but they could tell from Fann's signaling that it must be important. Once all in, they greeted Mr. Webster with all kindness and Miss Fanny closed the door and pulled up a straight chair just outside by the door. She didn't want to miss out on any drama.

Mr. Webster almost cried when he told the lawyers that the auditor of banks for North Carolina, Frank Gilmore, was coming back to audit vault assets. The lawyers quickly understood Webster's problem as the auditor would discover the substitution of the gold for the punk metal in the bags. Their idea was to top off the top layer with gold coinage that the auditor would not dig in too deep and would not check all the bags.

The bags were counted and marked on the outside so the totals could be calculated.

Next, the lawyer's angle was for Mr. Webster, if found lacking, and punk metal was found to treat it as an undiscovered theft. They asked who had access to the vault, and he did. Mr. Webster answered Susan Jackson was in and out of the vault most all day long, and yet another bank vice president, Robert Phillips. The lawyers advised to put the blame on Robert and Susan, accusing them of bank theft. That was the lawyer's advice for a backup position and since Billy Wayne Weatherman was running for Sherriff, possibly this would be a big case for him. Yet they did not think at the time about Susan's husband, Paul, as Deputy or her dad, Stamford Jackson, as Bank Director. Even though the people would be affected, Susan and Robert made obvious scapegoats. So armed with strategy, Eunicile Webster was calmed, and the lawyers reassured him it would all work out. They gave him a loan of which he signed for, gold coinage with which to seed the top bags and he put them in his buggy to work with that night after the bank closing.

Once locking up that evening, Webster opened the vault and sealed gold coinage on five of the top bags with new seals on the top. He then closed the vault, cut off the lamps and went home, doubtful but gratified for at least a secondary strategy.

Spencer Generase had gotten his wagon off Old Fort Mountain and decided to stop for the night in Morganton after telegraphing the confederate procurement officer Col Adolphus Mabry in Raleigh, he had goods to sell the army and would the service start a wagon toward him out of Raleigh to meet him in Winston-Salem for payment and transfer of the goods. Spencer asked him to reply to the telegraph office in Statesville with an answer so he could continue moving east and not languish in Morganton.

Miss Fanny was distressed at what she'd heard in the meeting between her lawyers and banker Eunicile Webster. She had gotten to her desk and written on a dictation pad the date and time of the meeting and an outline of what was said. She stuck it in her purse to take it home.

Tracker started again at where Socon Philip's body was found. He was headed further north this time, dog Skip by his side. Each step, the

Tracker looked for signs. It had been months, yet Tracker examined everything slowly and methodically. Was there any sign further to be had after all this time? As Tracker approached a split in the trail, the one he took up last time and the one down by the stream which entered below where he had found the shirt, under the rock by the stream, he took the left fork by the stream, carefully looking for sign. He got to where the rock over the shirt had been stacked, looking, looking, stopping, looking, and then stopped to rest a few moments and to pet dog Skip, who stayed right by his side. Sitting quiet, the birds began to chirp, and the squirrels began to scurry. The creek had yet to give up her secret of the murderous Indian who had been a passerby. Tracker made the decision to follow up on this trail and come back to the upper trail to examine everything that he could. Of course, he knew that a murderous brave would seek to cover his trail. So, it was expected to be hard. Why else would a tracker be needed for signs in the woods?

Manakee, the Oklahoma inquirer reference Sewakahony, had met with the North Carolina Cherokee elders and found that this brave had been on the periphery of tribal business and was a roving woodsman yet did have a small homestead place and did garden, but not for two years. He had not been seen. And so Manakee was ready to head back to Oklahoma but telegraphed back to the Elders a short report: Peripheral to tribe, loner and woodsman. Nothing derogatory to the character except a loner. Manakee headed south to the railroad station headed west train, and as he had fared, the trip back would be more pleasant. The jury was still out, so to speak, for Sewakahanee, who had settled with Eshamawa and now had a little son, Nevo Eva. (new start) Eshamawa was unsuspecting of Sewakahanee's crime as he was industrious and loving to her and their boy. There seemed to be no need in the house, and if a shortage came up, the problem would be solved within two days. Eshamawa wondered how things were going so well, but she was thankful. Her work in the clinic was gratifying, and again, if a shortage came up, it was solved in a matter of days. Life as it was, in Oklahoma, hot and dry, could not touch the beauty and green and beautiful waters of the Blue Ridge reservation. Sometimes, Sewakahanee got homesick for the beauty of his home, but he had murdered a man for hire, and that man's blood on the ground cried out for justice.

Spencer Generase got to Statesville without mishap and went to the telegraph office. Col. Adolphus Mabry said that he could not spare a wagon to meet Spencer halfway but would send a rider from Winston to accompany him to Raleigh and that they would buy his goods and wagon and stock at a premium price and buy him a train ticket back to Asheville. Spencer had to think about that. But that was the presentation on the table, and he hoped to liquidate his goods for a firm profit. Little did he think at the moment about getting paid in Confederate dollars. It struck him after he had answered the Colonel in the affirmative. He then telegraphed Kenneth Lee Oliphant, the liveryman, to build him a new wagon, which hopefully would be waiting when he got home. "Nothing in war or peace works out exactly like a man hopes for," he thought. "Sometimes we have to make do in the middle of a plan." Spencer had too much invested not to carry this through.

CHAPTER 4

Generally, Asheville in 1861 numbered in the city about 1856 people and of that, there could have been up to 30% slave population, which was the average percentage across the state of North Carolina. The fact that the characters in our story were well known to the townspeople was a feature of the small size of the town and the time and the fact that Asheville was more of a village and not spread out but had a concentrated business district. This familiarity led to easy networking, and with the large Baptist Church central to town and other churches south of it, the social fabric of Asheville was close to the fellowships in the churches. Though the recent secessionism had roiled the churches, ending up with a Methodist Episcopal North and South, for instance, the people generally that were left in town after the young men left for was coexisted until later in the war, 1864-65, when bluecoats from Tennessee and West Virginia began to press in on Western North Carolina. Here in 1861-62, the concerns were scarcity of manufactured goods from up north and crops in and around Asheville being protected from bluecoat raids.

Spencer Generese, the General Store owner in downtown Asheville, had embarked upon a trip across the state east to sell guns to the confederacy and his daughter, Kathy, was running the store. One Tuesday in

1862, Susan Jackson stopped by the store on her lunch hour from the bank and was distraught as the morning had been filled with accusatory questions from the bank audit team from Raleigh, who had come up to reexamine the bank records and had planned to stay for four days. They planned to examine everything there was to be examined, and the $500,000 journal entry Susan had made was the first glaring signal to prompt questions. Bank president Eunicile Webster had pointed to Susan as the one to address questions about directing Senior Auditor Frank Gilmore toward Susan, as he had been there previously and had questions. Eventually, and his audit team of four would count everything in the bank. This had Mr. Eunicile Webster in a bit of a sweat as he had moved the gold out of the bank and hidden it and, in the process, had the wagon driver, witness to the heist, Socon Philips, killed. Susan had no idea about all this. She had been concerned with working, rearing her new baby boy and getting used to handling the new confederate script, which had been the object of the new conversion first of the year. So here she was tearful in the General Store with her friend Kathy, who was commiserating with her. After a while, she had to walk the block back up the hill to the bank and get back to work. Kathy looked out the window after her, wondering why Susan felt so much pressure at work these days. Meantime, her husband, Paul Edgars, was meeting with Sheriff Billy Wayne Weatherman about the Socon Phillips case, reviewing where they were in it before he had a meeting with the grand jury and other case matters. Paul reported that they did not have a named suspect yet but that they did have a lead on the clan of the murderer and that he thought it might be a contract killing. His concern was that he had learned from Running Wolf that the clan, wind over the mountains, was thought to be extinct, but it seemed the found shirt, presumably the killers, had the symbol of it in the corner. This was a broad lead, but no person to bring to the grand jury. The Sheriff told Paul to keep digging, as Socon's brother, John Phillips, made an inquiry of the sheriff every Monday in an attempt to keep the case top of mind for the sheriff and his deputy. After the meeting with the sheriff, Paul decided he would go through inquiries again throughout the reservation and do it through Running Wolf in the quiet. Something might turn up. He would also have Tracker make inquiries in a concentric expanding set of circles from where the body was found and send him even out to Oklahoma if need be.

Evening came, and Paul headed home. He was anxious to see his little son Bradley Jackson Edgars and Susan, who got off at 3:00 to go home and care for the baby. Bradley was growing fast, pulling up on everything in front of him and an oncoming climber. He loved it when his Daddy came home, for he jumped and laughed and clapped for joy when Paul would come in the door and call his name. This was a great relief for Susan, who, after working most of the day, was trying to get supper on the table for both her, Paul, and the baby. It was a good, happy, warm evening in the Eggerton house tonight, and Susan did not plan on ruining it with her bank story about the inquisition the auditors had put her through.

Meantime bank president Eunicile Webster was closing the vault to close the bank for the night and the auditors went to a speak easy for a drink and a meal and then to a boarding house to their rooms. They planned to audit the vault in the morning unannounced all four of them. Bank president Webster had been worried about this but did not know it was coming on the morrow.

Kenneth Lee Oliphant, the livery stableman who had been frustrated with his attempt to sell horses to both north and south, was now beginning to get orders as the battles in Virginia ensued. He also was making custom wagons with high oak sides and high seats on the driver's mount. Here was the selling point: that the oak was less penetrable to the drivers and the wagon. He was getting some orders from both sides and was busy employing two carpenters sunup to sundown. Kenneth was judicious in his orders for Western horse stock as he had ordered too early and had high maintenance cost in the first sum of horses. He wanted to balance his orders against the casualties in battle if he could get the information. Kenneth endeavored to make contacts to get battle reports and try to interpolate lost stock. It was imprecise, but it was something. Kathy's Dad, Spencer Generese, had sold his guns to the confederacy and was headed back to Asheville, bringing cornmeal and flour, sugar and sorghum, and cooking equipment: cast iron skillets and billets of cloth. He also brought news of some of the first battles and stories from the men's confederate government. It had been a questionably perilous journey but a reasonably successful one. Spencer decided, though, that if he could hire someone for this job by job, someone he could trust or cut them in on his deal, it would save him time and wear and tear to pay the freight rather than the arduous travel.

Susan's Dad, Stanford Jackson, who had all the property and farms and mines and timber and slaves to work them, was having crops put in and canned in jars for his family and also for Spencer Generese General Store. Oak was going to Kenneth for his wagons, and the mining was of copper and hopefully sold, and what iron could be generated was going to the forge for sword stock. One of his black lady slaves was an herbalist who made tinctures for medicine, which Jackson bought from her at a modest cost and sold to the confederacy for medicine. He had a problem, though, in the latter years of the war, 1865-65, as Yankees had recruited black troops in Knoxville, and every now and then, one or two of Jackson's slaves then, would slip away and so his labor force (free labor) dwindled, not so a stranger would notice, but he noticed.

The law firm of Johnson, Wipple, Tayor and Young was seeking to profit from the war by investing in Northern Companies who had promise in steel, iron, woolen mills and railroad transportation. They had sold their southern habitational real estate holdings and were Yankee cash flush with gold to quietly reinvest. It wasn't that they were traitors it was in their nature to invest where they could make a profit. They did work for Stamford Jackson and others and had interests in a powder mill toward the border between Tennessee and Virginia and the burgeoning distilleries in Kentucky. Again, late after work, Bank President Eunicile Webster came down and met with the lawyers about this audit. Again, Miss Fanny was all ears.

The Elders in Oklahoma took their report from Jehewhanee about Sewakahony's reputation back east. He could tell there were secrets, but he was not told what, if anything, would impugn him to the Elders. So, he married Eshanamawa in good stead and began to prosper. The Elders, though, decided to keep a sharp eye on him and not to financially back any project he might propose asking for tribal resources. They loved and supported his wife, Eshanamawa's efforts in the clinic and decided that they would help the clinic, for everyone would benefit from it.

Cowboy Jeff Shrank in Wyoming was rounding up and green, breaking good horse stock as he found them. It was an open range and he could wedge a herd into a canyon and then quickly fence it and, select what he needed and let the others go. He sought to balance the herd and only took what would be a duplicate third of the catch. That way, he would be reasonably assured that he had a consistent source of horses to market both locally and to ship out. He maintained telegraph contact with the liveryman in Asheville, Kenneth Lee Oliphant, and they had a good and honest arrangement.

It was morning at the cusp of the continental divide on Black Mountain, and Sheriff Paul Eggars met Tracker at a designated spot overlooking the eastern valley below. Paul asked Tracker what he thought and what he proposed to do next. Tracker said he would like to pursue a railroad journey to Oklahoma to spy in that area to see if he could get any leads on someone who might have come there and prospered in the last two years. He would attend a council meeting and inquire of the wind over the mountain clan. He would dress very humblely, pretend to be impoverished and couch himself as a subsistence hunter seeking rest there on the reservation for a while.

The sheriff's deputy bought him a ticket to Oklahoma and a new set of clothes. He suggested keeping dog Skip while Tracker was gone, but Tracker said he would be going along. And so, it was set that Tracker was going into the lair of the contract killer of Socon Phillps unknown to him.

Chapter 5

One of Asheville's major challenges during this time of succession and war, and especially for all the merchants and those wishing to receive goods and ship goods to and from the region, is that the railroad had not been completed either across Old Fort – Black Mountain or up from Spartanburg. This meant that Asheville's lifeline railroad line came from the west, from Knoxville and as tracks ran, it also tracked north up into Virginia. When the Yankee sympathizers and later the Union Army captured Knoxville, then they controlled the line, and it was in constant disrepair from destructive attack and repair on both sides. Asheville had to be served by wagon from the east, and the Black Mountain range was steep and treacherous, an unrepaired wagon road twisting on a steep grade, challenging horses or mules or oxen pulling loads and even more challenging coming from Asheville east down a steep mountain. Even in good weather, it was perilous, with ruts, washouts, slides, and rock. This tended to isolate Asheville somewhat in the movement of supplies in and out of the region. There was good land gentler land to the south, and a road which was better south toward Columbia and Charleston, which was known as the livestock road and supplies from the South Carolina low country could be provisioned. From the mountains in Western North Carolina, southward, the farmers drove cattle, hogs, sheep, and goats to markets as far south as Charleston. And later in the war, troops from South Carolina came up to defend Asheville against Yankee troops coming out of Knoxville.

As a general store owner, Spencer Generase, Kathy's father, knew very well the challenges of procurement of goods for his store and the community.

He was blessed with local farmers for produce and light furniture to sell and his business relationship with huge landowner Stamford Jackson had a forge, of course, for the construction of hinges and horse-shoes and other items. Jackson was very wealthy, built on land and slave labor. His holdings were many and business was vertically integrated in agriculture, mining, timber, livestock, real estate and gold.

Spencer's recent foray east to sell goods to the Confederacy was arduous and took time. There seemed to be questionable profit in it.

At the bank, President Eunicle Webster was wringing his hands and breaking a sweat as the Audit team from the State Banking Commission led by Auditor Frank Gilmore began to examine the coinage bags, which had punk metal coins in them but were seeded with gold coinage on top. Mr. Webster, the bank president, prayed that this would be a cursory examination and that he would not be found out, having moved the true location of gold coinage to the law office of

Johnson, Wipple Taylor and Young then moved to a secret cave location on the Cherokee Reservation. Too bad, "he thought that Mr. Socon Phillips had been murdered." It just occurred to the greedy banker that he had Socon Phillip's blood on his hands and could be implicated as an accessory to the murder since he knew about it and had contracted with Sewakehomy to make sure the cave site remained secret. The realization of his trouble and crimes came down hard upon Mr. Webster, as usual, when perpetrators are found out.

The first auditor called for Supervisor Gilmore. "Look!" he exclaimed as he

S howed his supervisor the punk metal slugs in the bag under the coinage. Supervisor Gilmore bade the auditor be quiet and called the team together to quietly examine every bag in the vault before affronting Bank President Eunicile Webster. At lunch break, Mr. Gilmore went to the telegraph office and sent for a deputy state Marshall, which was a newly nominated office as the confederacy was running the government now.

The audit team had a quiet lunch, made their plan and went back to work. Mr. Webster, the Bank President, was the only nervous person in the bank. Susan Jackson, who worked for him, knew nothing of the gold heist nor the fraud and yet she was alarmed of sorts when Mr. Gilmore, the auditor, asked her if there was a photographer in Asheville. Susan, thinking nothing was wrong, of course, directed him to the photographer and Gilmore and the photographer conferred to come in after bank hours to take pictures of the audit found.

At 4:30pm, just before closing, Auditor Gilmore entered Bank President Eunicile Webster's office and told him he would need to stay over after hours for the auditors to complete their work in the vault. Auditor Gilmore did not indicate any irregularity at that time, nor did he announce that the photographer would be coming at a quarter till five. Indeed, in a few minutes, the photographer came, lugging his camera. Employees locked the bank, and Auditor Gilmore suggested that President Webster stay in his office so as not to interrupt the work and have them stay over longer. The auditors and the photographer went to work, flash, flash, move a set of bags, flash, flash, take a note, assign an evidence number, flash, flash. Three hours later, the photographer's work was complete, and the auditors had their evidence. At that point, Auditor Frank Gilmore came into Bank President Eunicile Webster's office and presented an order to seal the vault and to declare the bank compromised and insolvent, to be closed, pending further investigation as the bank had been embezzled or robbed. Mr. Webster blanched white but said little, as he did not know exactly what would happen next. As Susan had left early, she knew nothing of the trouble, and Mr. Gilmore put a sign up on the front door. After the door was locked, he placed a seal on the door. The bank was closed, and Susan Jackson Edgars would not find out until the next morning. Eunicile Webster presented himself at the local Tavern for the first time in 45 years. He ordered three shots of good Kentucky bourbon whiskey and downed them one after the other, to everyone's surprise. He paid the bartender and stumbled out into the night air. About this time, lawyer George Wipple was headed toward the tavern, having completed a long court brief in the office and met Mr. Webster. Webster told lawyer Wipple that their move had been discovered. They agreed to meet with the rest of the firm the next morning and went their separate ways: Banker Webster to home and Lawyer Wiple to the Tavern.

The auditors had a late supper at the boarding house and then

Mr. Gilmore checked at the telegraph office for the Confederate Marshall's reply and his arrival date and time. The Marshall, John D Proffitt, said that he had been in Columbia, S. C. and riding all night so he could arrive in Ashville by 8:00 am. It was confirmed.

Tracker had gotten to the tribal office in Oklahoma and introduced himself and his credentials to the tribal police there, who agreed to answer questions he might have about anyone who might have newly settled on the reservation in the last two years, and Tracker gave some detail about the Socon Phillips Murder and the shirt found and the clan symbol on the Mountain clan. The police promised discretion, and there was the quiet enumeration of the new families that had moved in and mention made of Sewakahony and his good f0rtune to court and win the most beautiful Indian Princess in the tribe and how together they had built up a nice spread and a good clinic for the reservation's people. Tracker asked about drifters, who had just passed through on the Railroad and would have just kept going. It would not occur to him that the killer would just move in, marry, and settle down in plain sight. The tribal council made arrangements for Tracker to stay with a bachelor of the tribe who had rooms to let, and he was gratified and settled in to clean up for supper. He was an investigator and not to be advertised. He was to report back, not take matters into his own hands and work through the law enforcement mechanisms already in place. Sleep came early to Tracker and his little dog. The train trip had been long and arduous.

Everyone in the community of Asheville was surprised by the closing of Asheville's main bank the following day, especially Susan, who had shown up to work on time and was sealed out. However, Mr. Gilmore, the auditor, was there to meet her and suggested they go for coffee with his team of auditors. Susan was confused but went and, of course, recognized that they must have found out about the irregularity at the bank.

Bank President Eunicile Webster was on the doorstep of the nondescript Law Firm of Johnson, Wipple, Taylor and Young as Miss Fanny came to open the office. The lawyers were about a half hour later coming in as they visited two breakfast places, networking, checking by the courthouse on the docket, and dropping in on some of their important clients. But by 10:00 am, the lawyers converged upon their own offices and found Banker Webster waiting in the conference room whereupon Miss Fanny brought coffee and pastries and the lawyers all sat down with Eunicile, and as the door closed, Miss Fanny left them but pulled up a chair just to the left of the door so she could listen. Eunicile, the banker, told his lawyer friends that they had been discovered and about the sealing Of the bank. The lawyers hatched a plan to one, set up an account for Susan Jackson Edgars in an adjoining but separate bank and seed it with $10,000. Then two, to plant a stash of coinage under their house to be found by whatever authority was to be appointed to investigate the outage. Eunicile was to claim ignorance and blame Susan, who was the head teller in charge of the vault. Miss Fanny frowned, as this sounded like a plan bad for Susan and her husband, too. She scurried over to her desk to make notes, and the men departed quietly; the lawyers went to their separate offices, and the Banker went to the magistrate to file a complaint against Susan. The best defense was a good offense, he reasoned.

Chapter 6

Now, it must be said that Tracker had never met nor knew anything of Sewakahony, the murderer of Socon Phillips. Even though Tracker lives on the outskirts of the North Carolina Cherokee Boundary, Sewakahony was a roamer. His and his family was south of the reservation. Furthermore, Tracker does not know that he was the killer, has never seen him, and has no real way to trace the evidential shirt back to him. Yet Tracker, during this search, had a little partner by his side on the trails of North Carolina while he was looking, and he had brought his dog Skip all the way on the train to Oklahoma. Sometimes, having a partner is good.

News from the magistrate's office to the Sheriff's Department travels fast, and Deputy Paul Eggerton got word that Susan, his wife, had been charged with the just discovered shortage at the bank. "That just can't be right," he declared and raced home to talk with Susan but did not find her there. Kathy, who was keeping their son, Little Bradley. Kathy said that Susan had left the house at about 7:45 and that she had to meet with the bank auditors. Paul went by to the magistrate's office to see who had signed the complaint/warrant and found that it was Bank President Eunicile Webster. So over to his house, he went.

Susan, in the meantime, was meeting with the auditors nearly at the coffee shop at a corner table, actually in front of the shop. Frank Gilmore, supervising auditor had picked the table to not arouse suspicion and to put Susan at ease, sitting with four men. He wanted things to feel casual at this point to be able to have Susan candidly and openly tell the auditors what she might know. Mr. Gilmore had no knowledge of the warrant that had been filed against Susan by Bank President Eunicile Webster. In their initial questioning, Susan told the auditors of her general office duties and how often the gold might have been audited; and, of course, her supervision was lax and the gold was cursorily audited only by the quarter. The head auditor, Frank Gilmore, did not show his cards or recite the problem that the gold had been stolen but mainly wanted to see if Susan was evasive in anyway or if this was a situation of casting blame on a lady who was of no knowledge of the heist that had occurred. One of the auditors was taking notes unobtrusively on a small pad as Susan talked. Of course, Susan was nervous about the interview, but as she had done nothing wrong, she was forthright and gave answers to all of Frank Gilmore's questions. The interview lasted about 45 minutes, and then the auditors bid her leave. Susan decided since she was uptown without the baby, she would do some shopping, have lunch, and stay till it was time for her friend Kathy to leave at 2:30.

Frank Gilmore and his men went back to the bank after getting Vice President Robert Phillips to let them in a side door and began to sift through the register of times and dates the vault was opened and closed and who signed. They already had an estimate of what was taken and the photographic evidence. Next, they planned to interview Bank President Eunicile Webster. Supervisor Gilmore dispatched one of his auditors with a written note for Webster to meet at the bank with them at 3:00 pm that afternoon. This auditor, Charles Mitchell, headed to Mr. Webster's home on foot. It was not far.

Susan's husband and Deputy Sheriff Paul Edgars had not encountered Eunicile Webster at his house because Mr. Webster was hiding out at his accomplice's law office. Here, the lawyers had ordered lunch and were conferring together with Webster on his story and what to represent to the auditors. Of course, Webster told the lawyers that he had sworn a warrant for Susan Jackson Edgars, implicating her in the heist.

Paul Edgars, Susan's deputy husband, stepped into the diner for a sandwich, and the waitress told him that Susan had been in with five official looking men and wasn't something to do with the bank closing? Paul didn't say much. He ate his sandwich and sipped his coffee, thinking about his next move, which was to go back to the Sheriff's office to talk with his boss, Sheriff Billy Wayne Weatherman.

The lawyers and Webster were reveling in the fact that they had gotten Susan's bank account set up with a little arm twisting and the bag of coins hidden under the house. They thought that they had set a good trap for framing Susan,, and it was likely to be.

Paul walked into the Sheriff's office after knocking and being invited in by Billy Wayne Weatherman, his boss and the high Sheriff of Buncombe County. The Sheriff, who never missed much, already had heard about what had come from the magistrate's office. Paul sat down, very confused, and the Sheriff said: "you know this has to be worked. But you know, I personally don't think Susan had anything to do with the bank heist. The question is what she might have known about it that would make her an accomplice". "Paul, he said. I am going to get you out of the middle on this and call in a special investigator, and I would advise you to have Susan be represented by attorney Sam Kitchens Esq in town, the one lawyer who has not been bought off". With this, Paul said he was going home to check to see if he could catch Susan and then contact Kitchens' Law Office which was on the west side of town and did have signage. Paul was greeted by a mature secretary who said that Mr. Kitchens was expecting him as the Sheriff had already contacted him by messenger, and then San Kitchens attorney Esq. with degrees from Ole Miss and Harvard invited Paul in, shaking his hand and offering him a chaw of good tobacco and sat down to talk. It turned out that Attorney Kitchens knew more about this already than Paul did. Kitchens had for many years. He knew the family well, had been to their home and watched Susan grow up. Kitchens was committed to defending Susan and, not only that, to get to the bottom of who actually was involved in the gold heist. The first thing he said was, "The man that throws the first rock is usually wrong, and Enicile Webster filing this warrant with the magistrate shouts of that" ... "But we'll get to the bottom of it. "Paul, the Sheriff wants you to work your current cases.

Have Susan come by my office at 11:00 sharp, and I will file representation papers. She has a little boy Bradley to take care of and a job to save, and I intend to help her,"

Paul left the law office feeling a little better. At least that much was done. Now, to find Susan.

It was now 3:00 pm, and Eunicile Webster came to the bank building side door to meet with the auditors. They settled unto the conference room that the auditors had set up with a board and an easel, showing pictures of the seeded bags of plug metal when the gold had been stolen. Also, was the signed record of the vault entry times and signatures Eunicile wasn't necessarily surprised at all this. He feigned shock and sat down, looking incredulous about the whole thing. Before Frank Gilmore began the questions, Banker Webster began to berate Susan Jackson Edgars and implied that she had done this with the help of her father, director of the bank and her husband, a law enforcement officer and that he was so certain that he had filed a complaint with the magistrate. Gilmore did not reveal that he already knew that and let Mr. Webster talk on. Finally, Banker Webster ran out of breath, and Mr. Gilmore began with his questions. He was still asking them at 7:00 that night. Eunicile Webster was on the hot seat, but the tread of proof was difficult yet to see. Gilmore had 20+ years of experience in these stories and had the convictions to prove it. He had put on a man to investigate Eunicile Webster's finances. It would take time, and that is what Mr. Gilmore had plenty of, Webster had less. The next morning, lots of people lined up in front of the bank.

As a matter of housekeeping, Mr. Gilmore had to send a telegraph to his authorities, all confidentially now, to set up a receivership for the Bank. This was done by the new Secretary of State and Banking Authority and sent back to Gilmore by telegraph. The receiver appointed was yet the third attorney entity in this story, David Potts Esq, practicing in Asheville, Memphis, and New Orleans. This was a comparable firm to Johnson, Wipple, Taylor and Young, but on the same level and capable of handling this duty. Hence, Mr. Webster was relieved of any authority he might have over the bank, and they could open tomorrow with hired staff from Potts and Company. What they were going to use for cash was Gilmore's next Challenge, but it was met with more confederate script printed to replace the gold coinage that had been in the heist. The next question was whether Susan could work as she was under a Magistrates warrant. It was decided that she could not.

CHAPTER 7

Tracker had reported in with the tribal elders on the Oklahoma reservation and was settled into is quest quarters, a pueblo just off the tribal gathering ground. Several had been built to house guests who would come for fairs, rodeos and powwows, and it was not a major distraction for guests to come, anytime, for a tribal function during any week. Now Skipper, Tracker's dog, came too. Skipper was a great dog that Tracker had raised from a pup. He was of an ancient Indian breed, dubbed the Carolina dog, which history tells us came over with the Paleo Indians across the land bridge centuries, even eons ago. Akin to the Dingo in conformation, this dog is short haired and pointed eared, smart and active and grows large enough to protect his master from most men or beasts. So, Skipper, the Carolina dog, was getting to know the sights, sounds and scents of this new Oklahoma reservation, keeping close to his master and trying to avoid fights with other reservation dogs who had territorial intent. To be a stranger in a strange land is difficult, and in the case of Tracker and Spike, doubly so, for they needed to circulate but be inconspicuous at the same time. They needed to enter the community and yet not bring too much attention to themselves. So, Tracker had to subtly ask his questions of the sort of down and outers on the reservation in the quiet. He would sit down beside them and ask about them, seek to make a friend and work the conversation around the question: 'Has there anyone that you know of in the past year settled in here? And the local would lead off and reply, "Can't say as I know," and then Tracker would drop the subject and pull out some ten dollar bills and hold them, folding them over and over, without saying much, and the local would look at the money and maybe open up a little... "There was one fellow who came in and lived here, north of town, on a small ranch with the prettiest woman in the community. Tracker would peel off a folded ten-dollar bill and hand it to him, thanked him, and move along. He would not pressure the locals but possibly pick it up the next day. As Tracker did not know what the killer looked like, he was at a severe disadvantage in this work, but he had to be subtle and humble and learn about the community quietly so as not to warn his quarry. A few days later, on hot, dry, dusty days in Oklahoma, a new poster went up on the tribal bulletin board as there was to be a Pow Wow Saturday night to celebrate the corn harvest. This happened every year, and its main purpose was to celebrate, sure, but to get the corn shucked. Men, women and children of the whole tribal community would come together for the event and, at sunup, would begin the drumming. There were huge piles of corn that were assigned to each clan in the tribe, and then there was a contest to see which clan could finish shucking their pile of corn first and claim Harvest Champion for the full year. In this way, the community could get a huge job done, and everyone in the area would be involved. Then, by four o'clock, generally, the job was done, and by five, a great spread of food was put out, and after giving thanks to the Great Spirit, each clan would eat together and rest for a couple of hours. The Powwow would be set to start at 8:00 as the sun was ebbing and it was cooling down. Women children, men and grandma's and Grandpa's all got on some regalia to come to Powwow. The champion shuckers were recognized, and a central prayer to the Great Spirit was given along with a song starting with the drums, and the Powwow would begin. There would be dancing until one in the morning. The children would start first as they would be sleepy and cranky if they had to wait, and the parents and grandparents doted on their show.

Tracker looked forward to taking all this in. He was looking forward to Saturday. In the meantime, he would make his rounds to the roadside down and outers and a local diner to watch the people coming and going. It was Friday in the diner when he saw her come in, beautifully striking, tall and winsome with long black hair and her clinical whites on. She got everyone's attention for her beauty, but she was unassuming and had come to get a takeout to eat at the clinic. Wind Blows Hair Across Her Face, surely was loved by the tribe for her gentle way with people. The tribe unconsciously guarded her as she, though not a queen, was loved as one for her beauty both inside and out. Tracker snatched his breath. He had not seen such a beauty on the East Coast and was glad he had gotten the chance to see her. "Now to meet her," he thought. The drums started early the next morning, slow working drums, and the people were out before sunup as the shucking had begun. Women, children, fathers, and mothers were all involved, for they knew if they wanted to eat this next year, this work must be done. Each clan sang their clan song as they worked, and then there were water bearers who brought water around the freshly shucked corn to the storage warehouse marked for each clan. Hands working, Tracker joined in the work, and Skipper stayed right by his side. Now it came that Wind Bows Hair Across Her Face and her little boy and presumably Tracker thought, her husband came to work. And when they got within 20 feet of Tracker and Skipper, Skippers head came up, and he sniffed the wind and began to bark. Skipper ran toward the man and jumped up upon him, almost knocking him down. Yet Sewakahony spoke to the dog and did not appear to want to attack the dog. Tracker got up and called Skipper back, who fretfully broke off the confrontational engagement and sauntered back over to his master. Tracker and the murderer's eye locked. They both knew that trouble was coming. Tracker stayed quiet. But after the lunch break, he went to the telegraph office and sent it to Paul Eggars, deputy sheriff, back home: Make the warrant come quickly. And it was sent. Paul received the telegraph, but he had problems of his own.

CHAPTER 8

"To go or to stay?" was the question the three men had to answer. For Senemawhany, the murderer, to leave would show guilt. For Tracker, to leave would be to go off the trail and give the murderer a chance to run off we're to be found again. To Paul Eggars, whose wife Susan had just issued a warrant for her arrest, to leave her in that situation would be the ultimate cowardice and dishonor and cost him his family. Sewakahany had too much to lose to leave. He had the most beautiful wife in Oklahoma, a nice little ranch and a son. If he ran, he would likely never be able to come back. "Besides," he thought, "The Dog can't testify." "Dogs jump up on people all the time," he thought. "They've got nothing on me." So, his decision was to stay and act as if nothing had happened. Tracker and Skipper were back at the Pueblo now and packing up. Tracker's decision was not to leave but to withdraw to an adjacent village for a while. This lets the murderer think he was gone and observe in stealth coming back to the village at night and in disguise. He reasoned that the murderer would not leave his wife and child for long, at least and maybe not at all. But it was Tracker's job to stay close until Paul arrived. Paul sat with the Sheriff and pondered what to do. The Sheriff had to act on Susan's warrant for her arrest, though he could dally a day or two, but it was there, and the

Bank President would be pressuring him to act. The Sheriff decided that Paul was to go out west, that he would not act on Susan's warrant until he arrested Sewakahany for the murder of Socon Phillips and Paul got back. There would be no dishonor then, as Paul was under employment orders undoing his duty, and Susan would still be free. The Sheriff figured that it was likely she was innocent; she wasn't going anywhere with their little boy.

Tracker went to visit the elders of the first village to thank them for their hospitality formally and largely. This was a courtesy but also to announce his leaving formally enough for the news to spread across the reservation. He was gone, he wanted all to think, and this was the best way to get the news out. At the elder's council there was a matter of ceremony, and the members and Tracker had to have a farewell prayer to the Great Spirit for safe travels and a smoke and finally Tracker made his way out of the village and was on the road to the adjacent, much smaller community, where he would take a job as a laborer by day and spy some at night and be as non-descript as possible so as not to spook his suspect into leaving and hiding. Tracker had figured that he would hide first, so to speak, and that was the reason he left. Tracker wanted everything in the first village to get back to normal, and he also wanted to leave the comings and goings of Sewakahany so that when the arrest came, he could be apprehended without a fight and with surprise. Paul, the Deputy, left the Sheriff's office to pack for the trip after getting the arrest warrant. He told Susan nothing of her coming problem but kissed her goodbye for now and kissed his son and rode to the train station on his horse and asked the liveryman to board him while he was gone. Setting in for the long journey west, Paul felt the train lurch and bump forward, and he knew he was lurching into an uncertain future. There would be a time when these three men would converge in the same space to determine each other's future. For now, justice for Socon Phillips was set in motion. Yet there was a war going on outside this situation, and many people's lives were affected in many mirid ways; some lost, some displaced, some running, and many dead. What would the war be to these three? It was yet to be said.

Meantime, from the east, another man climbed on the next train out west to Oklahoma and he wasn't carrying a warrant. He was carrying guns and knives. His mission was to follow Deputy Paul Eggars but not too closely. Nonetheless, there was a man who had a stake in the case. And as the trains lurched west, lives and fortunes in the balance, what was to come was any man's guess.

Tracker and Skipper made it to the outlying village, and he stopped in the clan's office to seek shelter. There was not a guest house in this little place, but they had a loft room in the livery up above the stables, and it had a straw tick bed and a dresser and a hole in the floor with a winch that could pull up a bucket of water for washing. There was an oil lamp, a pitcher, and a washing bowl, and the only rule was that you were not to smoke inside. As Tracker wasn't a smoker, this was not an issue. The place smelled of hay and horse and manure and tack leather, but Tracker figured as he would be spying, he would be sleeping outside most of the time. And so, for a quarter a night, which was highway robbery to him, he made his peace with it and at least had some shelter. This also played well into the laborer's disguise. Tracker unloaded his pack in his new bedroom to look for work. There was a community bulletin board, and jobs were posted there. It was farmwork or ranch work or mining or timber work. Tracker had his pick of tough jobs. He chose the farm work so he would have nights off and would not be too exhausted to do the spying he needed to complete at night and then work the next day. Tracker was strong and work mettle, and this came from an outdoor life and climbing all over the Blue Ridge Mountains since a boy. Like David the Shepherd of Old, this outdoor life gave him agility, strength and stamina, and so Tracker was well suited to do most any kind of work. Yet he was not interested in the mine work underground. And the timber work he had no experience in. Tracker went to meet the farmer after putting on the laborer's clothes. As he crested the hill to the farm and looked down into the valley, he saw the homestead and barns and livestock and paddocks and well, and on the right lower side, he saw that the farmer had a sorghum cane press set up by the stream where the cane grew. There was a Burro on the turnstile walking slowly round and round while two men fed cane between the stones to get pressed, and the cane syrup was being caught in large, fired clay jars. It could have been what it looked like now or a Biblical scene from long ago. But Tracker had done this work before back east, and he was confident that he could be of good help to the farmer. He and Skipper quickly walked down the trail toward where they were working. Upon arriving, Tracker began to help unload the cane, feed it into the press, and give one of the men a breather. He offered him a plug of tobacco as a sign of offered friendships and the farmer noticed that Skipper the dog was resting apart from the work and had sense enough not to get too close to the other dogs as it was not his territory, yet he knew they would eventually come to check him out. Skipper could fight to defend himself if he had to but did not go looking for trouble.

The day in afternoon was sultry in Oklahoma, and the water break was welcomed by everyone. Tracker again shook hands with his boss, the farmer, and met the two other workers, then he took a sponge that was for the purpose and sponged down the Burro to cool him off and save him a short drink of water. The Burro seemed to appreciate Tracker's attention, and after a bit, there was work to do before the sun began going down. The syrup in the jars was drawing bees and flies, and so the men tied muslin gauze over the openings and took the pots into the boiling house so they would be in the shade. This operation in Oklahoma was a day-night operation where the boiling off of the syrups was done at night under an open shed so as to be cooler work even though it was all night work. Tonight, they had eight mega jars to boil off, which stood about waist high and would boil off to be about a fourth of the original cane juice. But there was plenty of cane, and the molasses that was made was good and high quality and in much demand, and this was a sidebar profit center for the farmer and good eating on a biscuit besides.

So the men and the Burro and the dogs worked till sundown, and then the farmer's wife brought basket supper for men, and they ate and had a smoke, and the wife took care of the donkey and got him watered and wiped down and fed and stabled then took her basket and remainder picnic gear and headed back to the house where she would check the chicken coop for eggs and went in for her chores. Then, at 2:00, she would go off to sleep until breakfast time for the men. Boiling and stirring the squeezing's into syrup was just about an artform as too low a temperature and the squeezing's would not firm and too hot and it would scald a burn, so things had to be right and watched closely.

Then, the syrup was run off into clean large jars for storage and put into an underground cellar dug into the side of a bank and lined with rock and a thick set of twin double doors.

The men sang the Cherokee work song as they worked. It was believed that these songs, in a way, were religious and requested the Great Spirit to endow them the luck of the boil, that it would come out blessed and just right. The song thanked the Great Spirit for the stream and its banks and for the cane and the sun and the rain and the sugar in the cane. They sang thanks for the grindstone and the donkey and strong men and their wagon and the farmer's wife and their dogs and .... the barn cats that helped keep the mice out of the molasses. They sang of the corn cakes that were available to put the molasses upon. The combination of hard work and gratitude, faith and sweat enabled these Cherokee to be successful, for the Great Spirit and his sons were appreciative of hard work and gratitude. And in the darkness little wild animals such as raccoons and possums and bigger ones such as bars and coyotes smelled the syrup boiling off, and it smelled good for a mile in all directions!

In the meantime, at about 7:00 pm Oklahoma time the train with Deputy Sheriff Paul Eggars pulled into Tulsa for a switch to another train for the reservation. And another train stopped at midnight. It carried John Phillips.

CHAPTER 9

Paul Eggars, Deputy Sheriff of Buncombe County, who had a warrant for Sewakahany's arrest based upon a dog's identification, was reasonably aware that the tribal authorities would not likely arrest the murderer of Socon Phillips on this evidence and the fact that under the confederacy, extradition agreements with the tribal factions, had not been arranged. This was a long shot at best, and Paul was troubled about the bank problem back home and how long the Sheriff could hold out and delay the process on Susan's warrant, knowing that the Bankers could apply pressure on the Sheriff politically, but he did remember that the office of Sheriff was the highest authority in the county and that only the Governor and legislative could put pressure on the Sheriff politically and remove him other than the votes. This had not been done in North Carolina, and besides Billy Wayne Weatherman had Susan's dad's support, and he held great sway not only in the county but in the region and the fact that he was a director and major shareholder in the Bank. So, Paul had disembarked from the train and went to the livery to rent a horse to travel on to the reservation. He had been the only true tracker, and he made his indication with reasonable clarity. Though even yet, Paul nor anyone else except the dog knew what he looked like. As far as the reservation authorities, they would not want a murderer living in their midst if they knew it, and so they were at least inclined to listen. John Phillips, brother to the murder victim, was to arrive in Tulsa on a second train at about midnight. As this did happen, he too rented a horse from the livery and was going to stay behind the Sheriff Deputy and get lodging in a little village just north of the reservation and try to visit in and out of the main reservation town about every other day. He didn't really know who he was looking for either, but he could work on the periphery of the Deputy's contacts and eventually find out who the warrant was for. Now John Phillips had to have a story, and his cover was to be that he wanted to buy timber from the Indians for the confederacy and that he needed a guide that was local to go with him when he cruised the timber if the tribal authorities would allow it. He would employ Indians to do the cutting and transportation to the railhead and would pay them and the Tribe handsomely. Fact was that all this was fiction, including the promise to pay, but he wanted time to get around on the reservation without circumspection, and this was one way to do it.

Now Deputy Paul Eggars arrived at the tribal council building and police headquarters at noon after a two- day ride from Tulsa. He wanted to check in with the Tribal Chief first to establish authority and credibility, and the Chief was surprised to see a North Carolina Deputy Sheriff so far out of his jurisdiction and element. But he was curious and let Paul speak, and Paul, after presenting a letter from Billy Way Williams and the papers of the warrant, merely said that he had come far on official business and also asked where he could board for the night and find some vittles but that he needed to know about this man that Tracker's dog had identified and had anyone there witnessed as to who it was. The Tribal Elder thought it was ludicrous, for there had been nothing said about any encounter with a dog, and he had not seen it, and he told Paul so, but a young secretary who worked in the tribal office spoke up and said she saw the dog looking like he liked someone, but she'd rather not say who he was, for he was married to the beautiful maiden who ran the clinic.

The Tribal Elder reacted with quiet astonishment since he did not want trouble for Eshanamawa, the beauty of the reservation and resourceful caretaker of the health of the tribe. Therefore, he was very reserved and admonished the secretary that she had spoken out of turn. Yet Paul Eggars pressed for information about this lady, and finally after a quiet standoff of about 45 minutes, the Elder understood that Paul was not going away, and he agreed to take the Deputy to the tribal police authorities to get them to take on this situation. Since it was just next door, rather than taking Paul over there, he went and got their commander and brought him to his turf, and he spoke to the commander quickly to inquire but delay, inquire of the Deputy visiting, but delay. And so, the acting dance began a dance that had been performed many times between white man and Indians, and it went on for several days. Paul knew the game, and he was courteous but tenacious. In those wasted days, John Phillips made his way to the village north of where Paul was staying. Then, he got situated and began asking questions about who to talk to about timber. What he hoped to do was for the authorities to introduce him and sponsor a public meeting so that he could tell his story and offer the inhabitants jobs. That way, he could cover more people in less time.

Providence must have kept Deputy Paul Eggars and John Phillips apart for after four days, the tribal legal authorities said that they would hold Sheriff Weatherman's warrant and have the judicial council study the matter and rule on it to see if it was even valid and they asked Paul to telegraph his sheriff of that advice which he did. He received his answers: "Tribe is within their right to question, examine, and rule on the warrant. But you cannot wait for that length of time. The heat is on here on another warrant. Come home now. Billy Wayne Weatherman, Sheriff Paul notified the people he'd been talking to that he could not stay but that he and his Sheriff expected a ruling on the warrant in a reasonable length of time, and he left an address where news of the judicial council ruling could be sent and, that he was going to register the warrant in Tulsa with the State of Oklahoma and get a receipt from the Tribe that it had been filed what they gave and he bid them adieu and climbed on his horse, riding into the night back toward Tulsa, worn out and frustrated and worried about his wife and family and current job and future prospects for running for Sheriff. Paul rode without sleep through the night, camped and slept till noon the next day and rode all night again, headed toward Tulsa.

John Phillips finally got a day off from his farm work after they ran all the sorghum that they had to run. John cleaned up, put on new clothes and headed into the Tribal Office and visited with the Tribal Chairman of their Tribal Board to make his pitch on the potential for a meeting for a sale of timber by the tribe and the potential for jobs and a recurring income. John paid the chairman much respect and laid out a plan for the timber harvest and the wagon hauling to the railway in Tulsa. John presented himself well and then asked for a community meeting of people who might be interested in selling the timber and those interested in working for his company. He gave the tribal chairman a banking reference back in Asheville, and the chairman responded that a meeting announcement would be sent out for a meeting the next Tuesday at 7:00 at night. John bid his adieu to the chairman and went back to work on the farm. In the meantime, the chairman drew up the announcement, and one place he delivered the poster to be put up in the tribal rec hall, the Powwow grounds and other community settings was the clinic that Eshamawa ran and had an announcement board in the lobby. The chairman saw the potential in the timber contract for the tribe, to own thousands of acres or, you might say, claim the acreage. The chair realized that the civil war back east was going to create the destruction of property that would need to be rebuilt and railroad and barge traffic that would need replacing. Why not let the white man make war on himself and the tribe profit from it? There was seemingly a pleasing worry in this idea about the white man's conflict over the subjugation of the negro, much like their subjugation experienced in the Trail of Tears.

On Saturday, Sewakahony stopped by the clinic to see Eshamawa and to help clean and haul off the trash, which needed to be burned. He noticed the poster and made note of it, as on the back side of his small ranch he had a stand of good timber which was mature and needed to be harvested on a select cut rotational basis. Though Sewakahony obviously didn't need the money, he sought to use the ownership of this timber to get a foreman's job for either the tribe or the company to afford him the opportunity to legitimately travel the railroad back east to quietly check on his hidden gold and to see Hosekahony, his cousin to get news and also offer him a job on his ranch in Oklahoma. He felt like remaining too small in his farm operation needed to be sealed up, and with his treasure trove, he could easily leave or buy land from the tribe. Oklahoma was nothing like North Carolina in that North Carolina was green and rich soiled, and Oklahoma was dry in less rich soil. Sewakahony also wanted to look into the demand for horses from the continuing war. He was determined to dress in his suit and go to the meeting as a businessman rancher to present status for his family and get the job position that would serve him best.

CHAPTER 10

Kathy Generase was over at Susan Jackson Edgar's house, and she and Susan were watching little Bradley play on the floor with some toys. Kathy had just left the store for lunch and had brought some cheese and bread and a can of cling peaches, which were like gold as the army of the confederacy gleaned every field and orchard from Georgia up through South Carolina. These peaches were somewhat dated in the can but had not gone bad nonetheless and were "hum" good. Even baby Bradley liked them, so it was a peaceful moment in the Edgars household. As the war wore on, it was getting harder for Kathy's father to procure goods. He compensated by stocking local vegetables from the Jackson farms and cured hams and bacon, and he had some women baking pastry items for he had early on bought barrels of flour from up North before the secession, but just before.

Susan had been at loose ends since the bank had closed, but now it had reopened under a receiver, and she was hopeful that she could resume her routine of working until about 4:30 and leaving a bit early so that Kathy, who was babysitting Bradley could help her dad late afternoon and evenings at the store. The General Store was the center of the community for neighborhood news, war news and gossip, politics and other talk. It was no surprise to Kathy when today's relaxation and lunch were abruptly interrupted by a knock, knock, knocking on the front door. Susan answered it. There was a confederate Marshall, and he said he had a warrant for her arrest for theft of bank gold, and a search warrant to check her home.

It seems that Bank President Eunicile Webster had gone over the Sheriff's head to the confederate legal establishment to get a, for lack of a better term, "federal warrant served at the national level. Susan was put under arrest right then and there, and the house was searched. In the corner, under some wood under the house they found a bag of gold of small size but with the bank's markings on it and worth in the neighborhood of ten thousand dollars. Crying and distraught and in shock, Susan was led to a wagon and carted off to jail, but not in Asheville. She was taken to Statesville on an arduous journey, and Susan was so upset she was vomiting sick. Money talks and the banker Eunicile Webster had gone to the highest level to get this warrant served and arrest made before Deputy Paul Edgars got home. The Sheriff had sandbagged the local warrant too long, and Eunicile Webster and the town firm he was working with, Johnson, Wipple, Taylor and Young, conspired to get a confederacy warrant for the bank, which they did, though they were the very heisters of the money.

Kathy remained with little Bradley, settled him down and began to put things back in their place as the Deputies in their search had pretty much thrown everything around. Kathy got that work done, then packed up Bradley and his clothes and necessary things and locked up the house after leaving a note for Paul and took Bradley to the store, for she had to work, and she did not want to stay at the Edgars home further, and Bradley would be her house guest until Paul got home and Susan made bail if that was possible. Kathy stopped by her boyfriend's livery stable, Kenneth Lee Othario, and told him what had happened. She asked him to send a rider to Susan's dad, Stamford Jackson, with the news. At the time, Kathy had no idea where Susan was, but she knew Stamford would leave no stone unturned to find his daughter. Kenneth dispatched a rider to the Stamford home right away. Then Susan walked over to her dad's store.

Susan, after a day and night's constant travel, was placed in a women's prison in Statesville, given fresh clothes, some soup to eat and a solitary cell for now. Though the women's population there was not hardcore, Susan was sick to her stomach and near hysterical and needed rest. Her was a typical prison cell of the time, and once she got still and a little warm, she went to sleep just as if she had passed out. At this moment, no one from her home knew where she was. That was a bad predicament.

Paul had made the train in Tulsa and was headed home. He had two days of travel to go and was ready for a bath and a good home cooked meal, fresh clothes, and to see his son and sweetheart. He needed to report to his Sheriff and the county prosecutor, and he had no idea that Susan had been arrested and carted off. He trusted Billy Wayne Weatherman at his word but knew the warrant on Susan would have to be served. He thought maybe with Stamford's help and Susan's reputation, he could get the warrant squashed. He had no idea that another warrant had been issued by a higher authority. There was nothing to do about it there, on the train, so he pulled his hat down over his eyes and went off to sleep.

Susan had slept through the afternoon and night. It was like she had awakened in a strange new place. They brought her breakfast. Watery oatmeal, a slice of bread, and, believe it or not, coffee! It was not present, though, because she was going to be interrogated by the head of the bank commission at 11:00 am. Susan enjoyed her coffee, for she had no clue about her inquisition.

It was Tuesday morning on the reservation in Oklahoma, and as day broke, John Phillips got in his business suit, put his program information together and loaded three pistols: one in his belt, one in an ankle holster and one in a shoulder holster under his jacket. "Just in case," he thought and saddled his horse to ride to the Tribal Village to get breakfast and show himself around promoting the meeting.

At daybreak for Tracker, farming was his job with Skipper by his side. Tracker had heard of a meeting, but he had no idea who was running it or what it was about. He was going to the meeting just to see if Skipper had to reconfirmed any particular man as the possible murderer and to scan the crowd. It would be a goodly walk after work to get there but Tracker was invested in his quest to catch the perpetrator if he was there.

Sewakahony, too, was up to do farm work and help Eshamawa, his wife, at the clinic before he went, as they had a better way to bathe. He packed a fresh suit of clothes, shoes, and toiletries, and when opening his drawer, he grabbed his gold pocket watch and chain. He wanted to look like some form of a foreman and a little prosperous, though the watch had been gotten through ill gotten gain. It had beautiful, raised engravings on it of a county hunting scene in the forest with the hunter and his rifle and a deer in the distance. This was a the, last-generation watch with pure gold cases, and it was very showy. The chain was broad and flat and pure gold, too. It was a nice piece that grabbed attention when on a vest.

Eshamawa was working at the clinic. Today's emphasis was on giving shots and inoculations for children's vaccines for the next school term. Last fall, they had a measles outbreak on the reservation, and Eshamawa had applied to the tribe for funds for measles vaccine for this year. This was a new thing and she had lots of superstition to overcome in the giving of these shots. As the day wore on, everyone on the reservation was busy with their particular talent, weaving, farming, mining, medicining, tending flocks, and as the sun began to set, Sewakahony came into the clinic to get cleaned up and suited up for the meeting. His suit was that of a white man's style, blue-grey with a white shirt, tie, vest, watch chain, and watch hanging on the chain.

Eshamawa changed from her medical garb to a nice flowing dress, and they made quite a couple as they meandered down to the meeting house whose lights were on, lamps that are, and many people had come to hear about the new opportunity for Tribal Wealth. The Chief greeted everyone, and the chairman of the Board of Tribal Elders introduced John Phillips, whom none of our friends from the east had met, neither Tracker nor Sewakahony nor Skipper, and so this stranger to everyone there to explain how the timberland of the tribe would serve the confederate war effort and become a sustaining industry for the tribe.

John Phillips spoke and acted well, and the meeting was productive, with questions and answers. They took a break for refreshments, and John stationed himself in the refreshments area to speak to each person attending. It was when Sewakahony and Eshamawa walked up that first he was taken with Eshamawa's beauty, and then meeting her husband, he spied the pocket watch. It had been his father's. It had been passed down to his brother Socon! He recognized it, and his brain, working overtime, realized that he had met the murderer of his brother. Wasting no time, he pulled his pistol and shot two shots in Sewakahony's left chest. He then eased out of the shocked crowd, fled to his horse and rode south away from the predictable route that one would think he would take. Eshamawa tore her slip at the bottom to seek to plug the bleeding and sought to render first aid. She ordered some men to run, get the litter from the clinic, and to bring it. Law enforcement for the tribe farmed out in all directions seeking to track the perpetrator, yet it was dark now, and since the community had come to this meeting by horse and wagon, there was a hodge podge of treks, and it was difficult in the dark to discern which way John Phillips had gone. Two braves went wide of the area and began to slowly ride in a big circle around the village. They were hunting a straight set of tracks leading in one direction. Other braves went toward the obvious places, toward Tulsa in the east, toward the train station and toward the west to a stagecoach station line. Yet John Phillips was headed into the southern high desert. He had planned his escape and was headed south to Louisiana and an ocean-going paddleboat where he had passage booked to Bermuda.

The men brought a wheeled gurney to the aid of Sewakahony, and Eshamawa got him on a table and began to work. He was already spitting up a lot of blood. She began after giving her patient sedation, probing the bullet holes for the slugs. There was no guarantee of any miracles that night. The shooter was at large in John Phillips, and the murderer was in peril, tended by an unassuming wife. Life and death for both were in the balance. Tracker began a slow, methodical search around the building with Skipper hunting a familiar scent. It was not the shooter the dog led Tracker toward. It was toward the clinic. Enough, Tracker thought. This man is the killer. Too bad a dog can't talk nor testify. But John Phillips could if he lived to see the East Coast of America again.

CHAPTER 11

After five days of travel, Paul, Susan's husband and Deputy, got home from Oklahoma. He was wrank and needed bathing and a change of clothes and some good food, and he was looking forward to seeing his family, making up for lost time. He got off the train and rode into town across the hill up the road to Asheville in anticipation and hope of a welcome from Susan and Bradley and a good home cooked meal. He came upon his house, and nothing was stirring, he walked in and found the house so quiet. After riding the train for days, the quiet was palpable and as he walked around the rooms, things were not placed where they usually sat. He took it all in wondering. On the kitchen table, he found Kathy's note and Susan's arrest. He forgot about his hunger. He forgot about his clothes. He locked the house and rode directly to the Sheriff's office. Surprising the Sheriff's secretary by how rough he looked, he walked by and through Billy Wayne Weatherman's open door. Weatherman stood up and gazed at Paul somewhat apologetically yet said hello, and Paul reported his findings at the reservation about how he had served the warrant, how the tribe had stalled him, and how they would be awaiting the ruling of the judicial council. Then, he, in all courtesy, asked the simple question: Where is my wife? The Sheriff opened his top desk drawer and pulled out the warrant for her arrest. He had not served nor acted upon it. He had kept his promise. But for lack of better terms, he said that the Banker who had pulled had gotten a higher federal warrant, what we would have called a federal warrant in normal days before the secession and that a Marshall in the Confederacy served it, arrested Susan on the spot and took her somewhere, not sure at this time. Paul stomped around a bit and got mean eyed and determined. "Help me find my wife," he said and leaned across the desk while catching his breath. They both sat down to decide where to start. The Sheriff decided to wire the Governor to ask for help in the situation and then make inquiries in every county east of Asheville for each Sheriff. In a time of only telegraphs, this would take some time, what with the war going on?

Paul thanked the Sheriff and left, heading to the General Store to see Kathy Generase and his boy Bradley. Kathy explained to Paul just what happened. She did remember the name of the Marshall, and so Paul had at least that to go on, and Bradley hugged on his Daddy for thirty minutes and in the honesty of children, said, "Daddy, you stink." Paul laughed and said, "I'll have to do something about that". They both headed home, and Paul drew water for a bath, and he just got Bradley in the tub with him and they both washed up. Then they went to the café for a good meal. Once fortified, he took Bradley back to the General Store as Kathy had a bed set up for Bradley in the back room, and with a bath and a full belly, Bradley was ready to go down for a nap. Paul hurried back to the Sheriff's Department. He had a plan to ask permission to ride East to make inquiries. The Sheriff gave him permission for a week and weekend to be gone on this search, so Paul checked in with Kathy and went home to pack up for an extended search.

Sheriff Weatherman spent the rest of the morning at the telegraph office, and the operator burned up the wires, figuratively sending message after message to each sheriff in all counties east of Asheville. Kathy Gererase had told him that the Marshall seemed authentic and that there were deputies with him, so the Sheriff sent wires to every Marshall he knew.

Paul headed east. He spent three days stopping at every village, every town, every courthouse, every Sheriff's office and every jail looking for Susan. He had a picture of her, showing anyone who would listen and look. Finally, after zigzagging up and down from the central road, he stopped in Salisbury, which was next on his list and spoke to the Warden of the Prison. Paul was credible because he had his uniform on and his credentials and the Warden said, "Yes! We have your wife. She is under arrest for stealing from the bank in Asheville, and the Marshall has the evidence to prove it." Paul said, "then when is her arraignment and what is her bail?" He then asked to see her, and they took him to her cell. There now was a reunion of beloveds rarely seen as such in North America. And so, then Paul went directly to the telegraph station and messaged the Sheriff and Stamford Jackson and Kathy Generase as to where they were, that Susan was relatively well, and that Jackson and his lawyer need get to Statesville immediately so that Susan could be arraigned and bail set. This had gone long enough. Paul stayed there with Susan as long as they would let him.

It was a day and night's wait, and Stamford Jackson and his lawyer representing Susan showed up where Paul was staying in a rooming house in Salisbury and the three went to the courthouse to meet with the prosecutor to get the arraignment set up and bail set. It would take some time because the judge would not hold the court for another six days. This created a problem for the three men, including Susan. Paul knew he had to report back to Asheville on his job, and Mr. Jackson and the lawyer could wait possibly working on other things such as interviewing Susan for her defense while they were awaiting the judge to arrive and hold the arraignment court. This is precisely what Stamford Jackson and the attorney did. They met with Susan each morning and evening for times of two hours a day and went over every item of her bank job, the situation with vault supervision and the actions of Eunicile Webster. Also, the lawyer filed a motion for a change of venue back to court in Asheville, though he did not think that the motion would fly.

Paul, in the meantime, got home and picked up Bradley, got him settled in home and stayed two days with him under the Sheriff's permission, then had Kathy come daytime to his house to keep Bradley. In this way, he thought it would be less traumatic for the little boy.

Paul took his horse to the livery stable for reshoeing since he had traveled far. He also had them wash and groom her, give her some good grain and hay, and rest for a few days. He rented a horse with his Deputy's per diem and rode over toward Cherokee to see if he could get up with Tracker and any news from Oklahoma.

Picking through the rocks in the southern Oklahoma desert, or dry country as the locals called it, John Phillips was working his way south, moving at night and resting by day, heading to New Orleans while buying provisions on the way in each little village he might encounter. He had planned this part of a getaway, and the Indians were at a disadvantage because he had a good couple of hours of head start. He sought a southerly route with dry creek beds, which were rocky and hard to track through, and sometimes, he put buckskin pads over the horses' shoes so as not to make marks in the sand or rocks. He lit no fire at night nor during the day, living on hard tack and pemmican water, and in each village, he purchased a Jim Beam to fortify him. John Phillips was making good time, and since he had used an alias with the tribe, though they had put the word out in the shooting, it was the wrong name, and the tribe knew no different.

Finally, Thursday came and the Judge and the trial of arraignment for Susan and her father, Stamford Jackson and his lawyer. The Judge called the court to order, and the Bailiff called the court into session. Then, the judge read the warrant and indictment and asked Susan how she had pleaded. Susan answered not guilty, and the judge did award a change of venue to Asheville because that was where all the evidence of the heist was. Due to the fact that Susan had a little child and likely was not a flight risk, the judge set bail at $100,000, and Stamford Jackson counted out that amount in Confederate money, got his receipt, and he and the Lawyer hired a buggy, tied their horses to the back and headed west for home. The trial date was to be set one month hence. Susan was assigned to check in once a week with the Clerk of Court of Buncombe County, and she was free but under bond until the trial. The lawyer said that they had lots of work to do. Paul joined them upon their arrival home, and it was sweet halleluiah to have his family home that evening in spite of the coming trial and the hardships.

With Susan home to care for Bradley, Kathy Generase had time for a date with her fellow, Kenneth Othario, who ran the livery stable and had side deals with the North and the South to provide them horses for replacements for those lost in battle. Kenneth was really sweet about Kathy, and they had not been out for two weeks since Susan had been under arrest. There was a barn dance down toward the Biltmore area, and they decided that some good music and dancing might make a good prelude to romance later in the evening, walking home and stopping to smooch along the way. Hope sprang eternal in Ken's imagination, yet Kathy had so many friends from the store she had to be more demure about such things and guard her family reputation, so this wound up typical for the time's Victorian date no one would be critical of. Kenneth was hoping that his horse marketing to the war efforts of both parties would profit him enough to purchase a small ranchette just outside of town and have him ready to approach Kathy's father for permission in the old way, asking permission to marry Kathy. And Kathy knew of these plans and stuck right by Kenneth's side, for she loved the horsey smelling man because he loved her and would work night and day to prove his love for her.

Out in Oklahoma, Senakahony was fighting for his life under the operative knife of his wife, Eshamawa, in the clinic. In her haste, she noticed under his left arm a very small tattoo, which she had not noticed in their lovemaking. In was a circle with an inverted V upside down and two wavey lines over it. She did not know what it stood for, and she promised herself to ask him if he lived...

CHAPTER 12

———————

The day came in Asheville for Susan's trial to begin. It seemed like a David vs Goliath trial with Stamford Jackson and his attorney defending Susan and the District Attorney backed by the Banks prosecuting the case.

Jury selection took two weeks, for many people banked with that bank, and everyone knew Susan, so most of the jury came not from the uptown section of Asheville but from up around Weaverville and South Buncombe County. The jury pool was mainly of older men and women as the young men had gone off to war. There were mainly farmers, skilled workers and farm women on the jury. But Susan, as a town girl, now trusted them because she had grown up out in the county. The prosecution's main witnesses were Bank President Eunicile Webster and Vice President Robert Phillips, of no kin to either Socon nor John, a man who had moved to the bank from another bank down east. Though he had admired Susan's beauty from afar, they did not have much exchange at work because he was mostly in loans and collections. He did not handle vault matters and was basically the land loan banker there. There were, of course, tellers who had worked under Susan and the auditors from Raleigh and last, but not least, Miss Fanny from the law offices of Johnson, Wipple, Taylor and Young had contacted Stamford Jackson and his lawyer and declared she had testimony in Susan's favor. Susan agreed to take the stand. She testified she knew nothing for eight hours and eight hours the next day. Then, each teller testified, and they were neutral, not sticking up for Susan but not downing her. They were obviously job scared. The Federal Confederate Marshall testified to finding the bag of gold under Susan and Paul's house and the bank account across town. It did not look good to Susan, but finally, it was Miss Fanny's turn to testify.

Now, the Marshall had presented his evidence against Susan. Eunicile Webster and all the tellers had testified, and they were fairly neutral, but as we just said, they were scared. There were Susan's fingerprints among the bags in the vault that had been salted. It looked grim. Then, the defense called Miss Fanny from the law firm of Johnson, Wiple, Taylor and Young. In her little suit and little hat, she came tottering from the isle to the witness box, leaning on a cane, but her eyes were blue and shining like light in the darkness. The Bailiff stopped to swear her in, and she raised her little hand high and said that she solemnly swore to tell the whole truth, so help her God. Susan's defense attorney asked her how she knew Susan, and she admitted, even contending, that they were good friends, that she was friends with Mrs. Jackson and had known Susan since she was born. Susan's lawyer asked if Susan had visited her at her office, and she agreed she had. and then Miss Fanny took her little notebook out of her pocket and gave the exact date and time Susan had delivered a note to Mr. Johnson in the Spring of the year before. She asked the Judge if she could tell the jury what she knew to be true about this case, and she kept with her notes the day and time whereby Eunicile Webster, the Bank President, had come agitatedly to meet with the lawyers of the firm and that Miss Fanny had admitted to listening in on the meeting and that she was going to tell it all because Susan was a good person and did not deserve to be framed for something she did not commit and her notes would prove that on this date and that date and times the law firm and Bank President had conspired just after the secession of North Carolina to take the gold from the Bank vault and to move it to a place she did not know where. Then the Auditors, came about a year later, and on that date, Mr. Webster and the lawyers schemed to frame Susan for the heist that they had committed for which Socon Phillips provided the drayage and never came back. Miss Fanny read from her notes, whereby the firm planned and executed the setting up of the bank account for Susan across town an the hiding of the bag of gold under Paul and Susan's house.

Miss Fanny, with her good notes, stood up well to cross-examination by the prosecutor, and as there were no further witnesses, the case went to the jury. Susan, Paul and Stamford Jackson awaited the verdict with their lawyer, who advised them all to get lunch. Miss Fanny went to the law firm and asked a deputy to go with her. and gave them her keys and cleaned out her desk. She quietly left the firm she had served for nigh on fifty years. She then joined Susan and the group at the diner for lunch without saying a word more about the case. After lunch, Paul and Susan went by to see little Bradley at the General Store and to speak to Kathy, then they hustled to the courthouse to await the jury verdict. It came late that afternoon, about 4:30. The judge admonished, "What is your decision? Each juror was polled individually. The Forman first answered: To the account of theft of money from the Bank, "NOT GUILTY" To any of the peripheral charges, not guilty. Of course, the family and the community were elated, and they breathed a sigh of relief at the vindication of Susan Jackson Edgars. Miss Fanny was deemed a heroine by the community, and the Sheriff found a place for her in his offices as deputy emeritus and legal processor of warranty and papers of that nature.

Susan was released into the sunshine of her community, and the next month, Miss Fanny saw warrants for Eunicile Webster, Lawyers Johnson and Wipple and Taylor and Young for theft of money from the Bank. She also got an adjudication from the Cherokee tribe in Oklahoma refusing to honor the warrant for Sewakahanee's arrest based upon dog Skipper's circumstantial evidence. The letter did not address whether he was living or dead.

In April of the following year, Miss Fanny received a package from Bermuda in the Sheriff's office. It was from John Phillips, who had filed an affidavit that Sewakahony had killed his brother Socon not only because the dog was interested in him but because he had been wearing Socon's watch, and that was the reason he shot him. The package contained the watch as evidence and the sworn affidavit.

Tracker had since come back to the Reservation in the Blue Ridge with Skipper. He and Paul met several times. The watch prompted new charges against Sewakahony, which Paul intended to make stick since he was the new Sheriff, having won the election as Billy Wayne Weathrman stepped down at the completion of his term.

Chapter 13

S usan got a job as president of another bank across town, and trials were set for the bank president, Webster, and the lawyers. Bradley had a fourth birthday and found out he might have a baby brother or sister, and accessory to murder charges were filed against Mr. Webster, Johnson, Wipple, Taylor and Young.

The war ran on, and scarcities began to wear on the people of Asheville and their boys came back, some maimed, some dead, some triumphant. There were skirmish battles from time to time of guerrilla raiders coming from Knoxville. The home guard and troops from South Carolina came up to defend.

The community held together in spite of all these things, and in successful fashion after hard work of her sweetheart Kenneth Othario, Kathy got her ring.